⋆⋆⋆ Journey to ⋆⋆⋆
AMERICA

ESCAPING THE HOLOCAUST TO FREEDOM

SONIA LEVITIN

Aladdin

NEW YORK   LONDON   TORONTO   SYDNEY   NEW DELHI

ALADDIN

An imprint of Simon & Schuster Children's Publishing Division

1230 Avenue of the Americas, New York, New York 10020

First Aladdin paperback edition June 2020

Text copyright © 1970 by Sonia Levitin

Afterword copyright © 2020 by Sonia Levitin

Cover illustration copyright © 2020 by Violet Tobacco

Also available in an Aladdin hardcover edition.

All rights reserved, including the right of reproduction in whole or in part in any form.

ALADDIN and related logo are registered trademarks of Simon & Schuster, Inc.

For information about special discounts for bulk purchases, please contact Simon & Schuster Special Sales at 1-866-506-1949 or business@simonandschuster.com.

The Simon & Schuster Speakers Bureau can bring authors to your live event.

For more information or to book an event contact the Simon & Schuster Speakers Bureau at 1-866-248-3049 or visit our website at www.simonspeakers.com.

Cover designed by Heather Palisi

Interior designed by Mike Rosamilia

The text of this book was set in Adobe Caslon Pro.

Manufactured in the United States of America 0520 OFF

2 4 6 8 10 9 7 5 3 1

Library of Congress Control Number 2019949352

ISBN 978-1-5344-6464-3 (hc)

ISBN 978-1-5344-6463-6 (pbk)

ISBN 978-1-5344-6465-0 (eBook)

To my mother and father
And to my sisters,
Eva and Vera

★★ CONTENTS ★★

GOOD-BYE
TO PAPA

THAT WINTER HAD BEEN THE COLDEST and the longest I had ever known. It was a deep, chilling cold, the fog turning to rain, and rain turning to sleet and snow, until the streets of Berlin were white and silent. It was a strange silence, with people hurrying into their homes before late afternoon, as if the darkness itself might bring danger.

I sat in the window seat, my favorite place, for it was warm and cozy there, and I could see everything, both outside and in. Beside me lay my lesson book, with the arithmetic problems still unsolved. I had written only the heading, *Lisa Platt, February 7, 1938.*

"Are you doing your lessons, Lisa?" Mother came to ask, glancing anxiously down to the street.

"Yes, Mother."

We looked down together, neither of us speaking, watching the two uniformed men who strolled back and forth as if they were trying to reach a decision.

"If the doorbell rings," Mother began uneasily, then she said, "Never mind, Lisa. Just do your lessons. Everything will be all right."

How could I do my lessons, and how could everything be all right when Papa was leaving tonight? And what if the doorbell did ring, and those men asked for Papa?

I could hear my parents talking from the other room. "I've packed six new handkerchiefs for you, Arthur," Mother said. "They're folded inside your shoes." Since early morning she had been packing and repacking the two suitcases. Papa would take no more than he could carry, as if he planned to return.

Papa chuckled. "Now, Margo, don't you think they

★★ 2 ★★

sell handkerchiefs in America? You mustn't worry about such little things."

"I worry about little things," Mother replied, "to keep from thinking about the others."

"I know. Where's Ruth?"

"At her violin lesson—don't you remember?"

"I don't like her out so late."

"It's just past four, Arthur."

"I want her home!" Papa said sternly.

"I can't keep a fourteen-year-old girl in the house like a baby!" Mother cried.

There was silence, and I knew they had drawn close together, regretting the least little argument that they might remember after tonight.

"Are you meeting Benjamin at the station?" Mother asked, her voice gentle again.

"Yes. There's no reason for him to come here."

Annie burst in. "I want to see Uncle Benjamin!"

"Not tonight, dear. Papa's leaving."

Papa had left us before, two years ago, to get Ruth

⋆⋆★ 3 ★⋆⋆

from boarding school in Marienbad. We had planned to move to Brazil. That was the year the Nazis made the law that Jewish children could not go to public schools anymore. It was, Papa said, a sign of worse things to come.

Mother, Annie, and I had met Papa and Ruth in Italy; then we took a ship to Brazil. The heat in Brazil was unbearable. I was sick nearly all the time, and Mother, too, was miserable. Papa could find no work, for who wanted to buy coats in that tropical climate? So we returned to Berlin, and for a time it seemed that things might get back to normal, and that perhaps we had been foolish and hasty, as my uncles said, for leaving Germany in the first place.

But Papa had been right. Now the only way to escape was in secret, and the only place Papa wanted to go was to America. Who could picture America? I only knew that it was far, far away, and that I wouldn't see Papa for a long time.

I heard his footsteps and tried to smile.

★★★ 4 ★★★

"Ah, there you are, Lisa." He sat down on the cushioned seat. "I always know where to find you. While I'm away I'll think of you sitting here in your special place. But you haven't even started your lessons! What are you doing?"

"I've just been looking out," I said. He drew me close, and I shut my eyes for a moment, to remember this feeling.

"You must not neglect your schoolwork," he said seriously. Then he smiled and his dark eyes twinkled. "Numbers are the same, you know, even in America, so don't think your learning will be lost."

"I can't seem to concentrate."

"Sometimes we have to pretend, Lisa, that we don't see things."

"Like those two men? Why do they keep walking back and forth here?" I asked angrily. "Why don't they go away?"

"They're going now," Papa said. "See? There was nothing to worry about at all."

"Maybe that's what the Mullers thought," I said, immediately wishing I had not spoken.

"What do you know about them?" Papa asked, startled. "You hear everything, don't you?" He sighed, but in an instant his eyes were gay again. "Sometimes I forget that you're not a little girl anymore. When did that happen?" he teased. "Wasn't it just a few days ago that I came home from work and Frau Leuffelbein met me at the door and said, 'Dear me, another girl. Oh, I am sorry!'"

I laughed in spite of myself. "That was when Annie was born."

"Oh yes," he said. "Now I remember. Poor Frau Leuffelbein—she had promised me a boy that time. She was quite shocked, I recall," he laughed.

Papa was always teasing about Frau Leuffelbein and about having all girls. "If I had ten children," he would say, "you can bet they'd all be girls." But he always carried our pictures with him in his wallet and showed them around to everyone.

Now he spoke seriously, "I'm depending on you to help Mother while I'm away. You're so good with Annie, and I know you can take responsibility. And please, Lisa, don't worry Mother by talking about things like—like the Mullers."

"I won't, Papa. I'll be cheerful."

"Good! You're rather pretty when you smile, you know."

Annie came running in. "Am I pretty too?"

"You—you're a little clown!" Papa scooped her up in his arms and tickled her until she squealed, then he put Annie on his shoulders the way he used to do with me. Just then Ruth came in, with her cheeks red from the outside, and Mother tried to get us all settled down for supper.

"Stop playing, Arthur," Mother said, concealing a smile. "You're worse than the children. Go wash your hands, Annie. Ruth, you're dripping water on the rug. Lisa, ask Clara if dinner's ready."

"An organizer, that's what your mother is," said

Papa. "Look at her, children! A fabulous woman—beautiful . . ."

"Oh, hush, Arthur. Come to dinner."

Clara had been cooking furiously all day, and scrubbing and cleaning in between. It was her way, when she was troubled, to keep her hands busy.

For dessert Clara had made Papa's favorite, plum cake.

"Clara, you're a genius!" Papa exclaimed. "How did you find plums in winter?"

"You can get anything for a price," Clara said, then she quickly excused herself, and I saw that there were tears in her eyes.

Clara was like a second mother to us. She had been with us ever since Ruth was little, and when we returned from Brazil she was waiting at the station. "Frau Platt, you are like my own family," she always said.

Even when the Nazis made the law that Christians could not work for Jews, and the penalty was imprisonment, Clara refused to leave.

"I'm not afraid of them and their laws," she said, and her voice bristled with defiance.

"But I'm worried about you, Clara," Mother said. "You should find yourself another place."

"You think I'm like that Marie, to run off like a scared rooster?" Clara said. Marie had been hired to do the housework, while Clara looked after Annie and did the cooking. Now that Marie was gone, Clara's work was doubled, but still she remained firm.

"Oh, Clara, what's to become of you?" Mother sighed. "I think you'd thumb your nose at the devil!"

"Perhaps not at the devil," Clara laughed, "but at Herr Hitler, you can be sure!"

I tried to forget that Papa was leaving tonight, to pretend that it was an ordinary evening. But all through the meal I felt that I was just listening and watching, that I wasn't really a part of it.

"Lisa, you're dreaming," Mother said. "You haven't even touched your cake."

"I'll have it later. I'll go help Clara with the

dishes." I purposely pushed aside the thought of my arithmetic homework. I wanted to be with Clara, watching as she washed the dishes in a large pan filled with suds. She worked vigorously, but she talked in a gentle, easy way.

"Ah, Lischen, you've come to help me," she said. "I was wishing for company. Tell me, did you have dancing at school today?"

"No. Tuesdays and Thursdays. I don't want to talk about school."

"So. Are you going to cry?" Her look was direct and challenging.

"If it weren't for Uncle Benjamin," I said, "Papa wouldn't be leaving."

"That's nonsense," Clara retorted. "Who told you that?"

"It was Uncle Benjamin's idea for him and Papa to go to America together."

"Your father didn't need anyone to tell him. It's the only wise thing to do."

"Then why aren't the others leaving?" I demanded. My grandparents, uncles, aunts, and cousins—all were staying in Germany. "Rosemarie says that her parents say there's nothing to get upset about," I went on heatedly. "They say that nobody should take Hitler seriously, and it's silly for people to move away, because it will all blow over."

"It's far more silly for people to ignore what's going on right under their noses!" Clara exclaimed. "Your father is just smarter than the others," she continued, "and he has courage. Don't you think it takes courage to give up everything, his home, his business, and to start all over again in a strange country? You," she said sternly, "should be proud of your father."

"I am!" I cried. Already I felt empty inside, as if Papa had left. "I'll miss him," I whispered. "And what if they stop him at the border?"

"Now, now," Clara soothed. "I know you're thinking about the Mullers. *I* know you listen to everything. But think, Lisa. The Mullers were arrested because they were trying to smuggle out money."

"It was *their* money! It doesn't make sense. . . ."

"They broke the law."

"What kind of law is that?" I demanded.

Clara sighed deeply, then she wiped her hands on her apron and turned to me.

"How can I explain it? I don't even understand it myself. What kind of law? you ask me—an evil law, that's all I can tell you. Laws should be for the good of people, not against them. But these are terrible times."

I knew that the Nazis hated us, and only because we were Jews. But why? What had we done? One of the laws was that Jews could not take money out of the country. The Gestapo, the secret police, saw to it that Hitler's laws were enforced.

The Gestapo had searched the Mullers at the border, even taking the baby from Frau Muller's arms to look through its clothing. Under the little vest they found a bundle of bills, and the Mullers were taken off to jail. What became of the baby, I didn't know.

"Your father won't take any chances," Clara said. "He is a clever man. And soon you'll be going. Think of it!" Her eyes shone. "Oh, what I wouldn't give to go to America!"

"Come with us then," I begged, flinging my arms around her. "Oh, please, Clara."

"No, Lischen, I can't. My mother is too old to travel, and I'm the only one she has. Go now. Your father wants to talk to you. And don't show such a long face!"

I went into my parents' bedroom. Papa's suitcases stood by the door; his overcoat and briefcase were laid out on the chair. I watched while Papa combed his hair, then patted his cheeks with shaving lotion and fastened his cuff links. I always liked watching him. When I was little he used to dab my cheeks with the foamy soap from his shaving brush. Then he would laugh. "Oh, pardon me. I forgot you're too young to shave."

When Mother and Ruth came in, Papa said, "Time now for talk, then for presents."

We sat on the bed, Mother and Ruth and I, and Papa pulled over a chair.

"Ruth," he said, frowning, "I'm going to have to ask you to make a sacrifice."

Ruth flushed slightly and stared at Papa.

"I'm afraid that you are going to have to interrupt your violin lessons for a while."

"But Papa!" Ruth began to twist the dark lock of hair on her forehead.

"I know how much it means to you, but you cannot be out alone so late in the afternoons," he said. "And I don't want your mother to be worrying about you."

"All right," Ruth whispered, and then she glanced at me as if to say, *Now, what will* you *sacrifice?*

There was nothing for me to give up. I had stopped taking ballet lessons from Frau Zimmerman more than half a year ago. "She cannot teach you anymore," Mother had told me, and I didn't ask why.

Papa leaned forward in his seat. "I want you to listen closely now. Listen well, and remember. I am going to send for you. As soon as possible, we will be together in America."

"When?" I whispered, almost frightened by the look in Papa's eyes.

"Soon," Papa said. "Don't ask me more. Ruth and Lisa, I am going to ask you for the most important promise you have ever made. You must not tell anybody about our plans, not even your closest friends. Promise me."

Together we promised, Ruth and I, and my heart was thumping as if, in some strange ritual, I had sworn a sacred oath in blood.

"It will take time," Papa continued, "for me to get settled in America and to make the arrangements. When it is time for you to leave, you will tell nobody where you are going. It will be as if you were only going on a short vacation, to Switzerland or to France."

"But how can people think that," Ruth asked, "when we'll be moving out?"

"You won't move out," Papa said, his hand uplifted for attention. "Everything will be left here."

"Everything?" I echoed.

"Yes," said Papa, "except for your clothes and personal things. But listen! The most important thing is that you must obey your mother, immediately and without question. Your lives," he said, "could depend on it."

"You are frightening them, Arthur," Mother said in a low tone.

"Better to frighten them," said Papa sternly, "than to take chances." He reached into his pocket, and in that instant his eyes were gay again. Papa loved giving presents, I think, as much as we loved receiving them.

We knew that he had no patience with wrappings and strings. "Close your eyes," he said, "and hold out your hands."

When I opened my eyes, there was a ring on my

finger so deeply red and glowing that it seemed to warm my whole hand. I couldn't even think to say thank you—I only gasped, while Ruth exclaimed, "Oh, thank you, Papa. Thank you!"

I saw that on her hand was a ring like mine, except that the stone was bright green.

"I'm glad you like them," Papa said, chuckling. "You have good taste. These are real," he added, taking each of our hands into his own. "Your stone is an emerald, Ruth, and yours, Lisa, is a ruby. But we'll pretend that they are only glass. That is another secret we'll keep between us." He turned to Mother. "You could sell these anywhere, if necessary, and get a fair price."

"You mean we won't keep them?" Ruth asked, and I could see that she was close to tears, for she pulled at the curl on her forehead.

"You'll keep them," Papa replied, "unless your mother needs them. Then, of course, you must give them to her. You are to wear these always," he said, "from the time you leave Germany until we are together again. That way you won't lose them."

Papa looked at his watch. "It's time to say good night."

It was the moment I had dreaded all day, and I saw Ruth go calmly to kiss Papa, as if tonight were like any other. I wondered why Ruth didn't feel as I did that terrible tightness inside. Or did she? Did she, too, hold back a cry? *Don't leave me, Papa. Don't go!*

I kissed Papa's cheek, and he put his hand on my hair for a moment, holding me close. "Good night, Lisa," he said, and then he whispered close to my ear, "God keep you."

For a long time after Ruth's breathing had grown deep and even, I lay awake listening to the sounds in the house. Finally I heard the front door close. Papa was gone.

PROMISES
TO KEEP

THROUGH THE LONG DAYS OF WAITING TO hear from Papa, Mother was calm. But when we received the telegram, ARRIVED SAFELY, ALL IS WELL, tears rolled down Mother's cheeks.

Since Papa had left, relatives came to visit every night, hoping for news, giving advice.

"Now that Arthur's gone, they might suspect something," my grandmother said. "Maybe you should send the children ahead to England, Margo. At least they would be safe. Many people are doing it."

"I won't do anything without consulting Arthur,"

Mother always said firmly. "The children and I will stay together."

"I'll be glad to keep Annie with me when you leave," Grandmother Platt offered. "Don't you think she's too young for such a trip?"

"No," Mother said. "I couldn't leave her."

Always their conversations turned, finally, to "the question." Then their voices were hushed and they glanced about as if the very walls had ears. How much longer should they wait? How much longer would it be safe for them to walk the streets of Berlin? Wouldn't someone, somehow, bring this madness to an end?

I tried not to listen. I wished I could be like Ruth, always in the midst of a good book or off on some project. Instead, I found myself hearing and knowing more than I wanted to. Every day brought new incidents.

"Isaac Cohn's store windows were smashed today. He's talking about leaving for China."

"Helen Kraus told me they came for her husband early this morning. They took him for 'questioning.' You know what that means."

"People won't come to my store since the Nazis painted that sign on the wall. 'I can't buy from Jews,' one man told me. 'Nothing personal, you understand.'"

Despite everything, Mother said we were to act natural. We told Annie nothing of our plans. She was too young to be trusted, and too much of a chatterbox. We didn't even tell her that Papa would send for us. She believed that he was coming back.

Late in March Papa wrote that we must prepare to leave Germany as soon as possible. Hitler's armies had marched into Austria. We sat huddled by our radio listening to that thundering voice. "My German comrades, Austria is ours! It is only the beginning. It will come to pass, my comrades, as I have promised. Germany will rule the world!"

Even in his letter, Papa was careful to reveal nothing, for nobody questioned the actions of the

Gestapo anymore. They could and did barge into homes and restaurants, hauling people away without explanation. They could and did inspect the mail to learn the names and intentions of those who were "unfriendly" to their cause.

"I think it would be a good idea," Papa wrote guardedly, "for you to take the girls to Switzerland for a short vacation. Make all the arrangements, Margo, and write me of your plans."

"When are we leaving?" I asked Mother again and again, and she always shook her head. "I'm not sure. There is so much to do."

"May I tell Rosemarie that we're planning a vacation?"

Mother hesitated, then nodded. "I suppose we might as well tell our friends, but only that we're going on a vacation. It would be the natural thing to do."

I had not shown Rosemarie my ring, afraid that I might reveal something. We had never had any secrets before.

I told her at school one day, while we were sitting on the bench waiting for Frau Meyers, the ballet teacher. "I think we'll be going on a vacation soon, Rosemarie."

"That will be nice," she said, smiling. "Where?"

"To Switzerland, I think."

Just then Hanna Hendel came up, smiling in her mysterious way and shaking her head to make her curls bob. "Have you heard?" she said breathlessly. "Have you heard about Eleanor?"

"No," I said, tired of Hanna's endless gossip.

"Nobody's supposed to know," Hanna said, "but Eleanor and her family have left for good. Don't you want to know how I found out?" She looked at Rosemarie and me, wanting us to coax her to tell, but we kept our faces blank.

"I know you're dying to tell us," Rosemarie said.

"Well, our Lucy knows the woman who worked for Eleanor's parents," Hanna said, flushed with eagerness, "and she told Lucy that they are going to America."

I looked down at the floor, so that Hanna would not guess how I felt at hearing the word "America."

"I wouldn't want to go to America," Hanna went on. "They speak French there, you know, and who wants to have to learn French? I'd hate it."

We didn't even correct her. I was too disgusted by her gossip and her hating things. She hated school; she hated Frau Meyers and the ballet lessons, and I think she hated me. Maybe it was because Frau Meyers said I was the best dancer in the class, and Hanna couldn't stand to take second place. She had a way of finding people's weaknesses and picking on them. Even on my first day at school, she had noticed the scar on my leg and asked rudely, "Where did you get that scar? Were you in an accident?"

"I had an infection there," I told her. "It happened when we were in Brazil." I really didn't feel like talking about it.

"How awful!" she gasped. "You'll always have to wear thick stockings. I hate thick stockings, don't you?"

It was then that Rosemarie came up to me and, smiling, introduced herself, and warned me about how unpleasant Hanna could be. It was the day that Rosemarie and I became best friends.

Now I told Rosemarie, "We might be leaving even before school is out. Mother is going to see about our passports today. I just want to tell you . . ."

"Don't tell me anything," Rosemarie said quickly, taking my hand. "Just give me a picture of yourself that I can keep while you're in Switzerland. Look, here's Frau Meyers. Let's get in line."

There is something about dancing that makes me forget everything else. I feel free then, as if I am flying. How I love the feel of ballet slippers on my feet!

But it was to be the last dance lesson. Frau Meyers was leaving. One by one the teachers were leaving, without explanation. We had learned to ask no questions, knowing that answers were impossible to give.

"Don't ask any questions," Mother told me again that afternoon when we were on our way to the passport office. "Don't talk, unless you are spoken to."

Ruth had decided to stay home and practice her violin, and Annie was napping. I had begged Mother to let me come with her.

"I'm glad you're with me," Mother admitted as we stood before the large office building. "Are you afraid?" she asked.

"No. I am *not*." But my heart was pounding when we walked through the door.

The man behind the desk had a square, strong face. He breathed heavily, through his mouth, and his thick fingers were busy among the papers on his desk. "Well?" he said without looking up. "What do you want?"

"I have come to pick up my passports," Mother said, and I marveled that her tone was so calm and even. "Here is the receipt showing that we have paid all our taxes."

"Why do you want to leave Germany?" he demanded.

"My children and I have planned to take a short vacation in Switzerland. You will see that all my papers are in order."

Mother handed him the tax receipt, and as I glanced at it I saw a word printed across the top in bold red letters, *Jude*, Jew.

The man glanced at the papers, then looked fully at Mother. "Your papers are definitely *not* in order," he said, breathing deeply. His face was red from some great effort. "I cannot give you a passport." He waved his hand and called loudly, "Next!"

"But I have everything ready," Mother said patiently. She pressed my hand tightly, warning me to be still.

"You had a passport before," he declared. "What happened to it?"

"It was taken from me two years ago," Mother answered, "when I returned to Germany from Brazil."

"So!" His breath was a hiss, and his eyes seemed to bulge from his face. "People have been known to sell their passports. We have strict rules . . ."

"Oh, Karl," came a loud voice from the back of the room, and I jumped, not having noticed that anyone else was with us. Now a tall young man came forward. "Why are you making such a fuss about this?" he asked, grinning and shaking his head. "Can't you see this woman just wants to take her children on a little holiday? I can't blame her—it is a superb time to go."

He smiled at me, and I struggled to return his smile.

"But you know the rules, Fritz," the other man objected.

"Her passport was taken by our own officers," the young man said impatiently. "Don't you see the notation here?" He pointed to one of the papers. "Come on now, and don't take all day about it. We'll miss our afternoon coffee."

"Then you must take the responsibility," said the other stiffly. "I refuse to be responsible." But as he spoke he took a slim green book from his desk drawer, stamped it several times, and handed it to

Mother. "The children," he said gruffly, "can go on your passport."

"Thank you," Mother said briskly, and I kept my face rigid, as if I didn't really care.

"You are allowed to take out ten marks for each person," the man said.

"Ten marks!" Mother's eyes were plainly troubled. "I thought it was more."

"Ten marks," he snapped. "The rules change, you know."

"Have a pleasant holiday!" the young man called after us. And as we left I heard him say, "Oh, Karl, you are getting so suspicious," to which the other replied, "But, Fritz, they are Jews."

Ruth and Annie were sitting on the front step waiting for us when we got home. "There's a man in the living room!" Annie cried happily.

"Did you get it?" Ruth asked. Her tone was low and urgent.

"Yes, dear. But who is here?"

"Herr Mendel," Ruth replied. "We didn't know whether to let him in."

"He insisted on seeing you," said Clara softly, "and Ruth told me you know him, so I thought it was all right."

"Yes, I know him," Mother said. "My husband did business with him. But what could he want?"

I followed Mother into the living room. I had left a book on the window seat, and now I went there, as if to read. The drape was half closed, and I sat very quietly with the open book on my lap.

Herr Mendel did not even seem to notice me, although he had been very nice the day Papa took me to his shop. Herr Mendel made the patterns for the coats that Papa designed. I remembered seeing the stacks of bright cloth that were cut into peculiar shapes, bits of wool and silk that were left over. Herr Mendel gave me a sack full of the scraps to take home to use for making doll clothes.

He had smiled at me then, and I had thought

how much his little mouth resembled a prune, for he barely moved his lips, and I had very nearly laughed aloud.

Now he spoke in a different voice as he faced Mother. "I have come for the money your husband owes me."

Mother walked toward him slowly, then she stood beside the easy chair, as if to steady herself. "My husband," she said firmly, "owes you nothing."

For a moment they only looked at each other, Herr Mendel with his eyes narrowed, as if he were judging Mother's strength.

"I know that my husband paid all his accounts before he left," Mother continued, holding her ground.

"He never paid me for the last delivery," Mendel insisted. He took a yellow piece of paper from his vest pocket. "You see? Here is the order form. Check it for yourself."

"The order is right," Mother said, "but apparently

you forgot to mark that it was paid. My husband always pays his bills on the first of the month. In all the years he has worked with you," she said heatedly, "you have never had to come and ask for your money. Isn't it true?"

"My dear Frau Platt," said Mendel smoothly, "I have no doubt that it was an honest mistake. Probably in the excitement over his trip, your husband simply forgot to pay me. His plans were rather sudden, weren't they? It's not as if I am desperate for the money. I have, in fact, a large contract from the government to make uniforms. So you see, I am on good terms with the Nazis."

"I see," Mother whispered, blinking rapidly.

"Everyone knows your husband has left," he continued. "It might be difficult for you, unpleasant indeed, if I had to go to the police about this. It's only a small matter—two hundred marks. I'm sure your husband would want you to pay it—under the circumstances."

"Wait here," Mother said. All the color had gone from her face, and I could see her anger in the way she walked.

When Mother was out of the room, Herr Mendel moved toward me. He smiled with his thin lips pursed and held out his hand, but I could not make myself go toward him. "How are you, my dear? I suppose you miss your Papa. He and I have always been good friends. Are you going to see him soon?"

My throat was so dry I couldn't have spoken had I wanted to. I wondered whether he could see in my face how I hated him, and I wished desperately that I had never taken his gift, that bag of brightly colored scraps.

"Here you are, Herr Mendel," Mother said stiffly, and she watched him as he counted the money. "You may give me that order form as a receipt."

"Gladly," Mendel replied, smiling. "I want everything to be done properly. Everybody knows how I do business."

★★ 33 ★★

"I'm sure," Mother said, taking him to the door and closing it swiftly behind him.

Mother sank into a chair, breathing heavily. "Call Clara," she told me, and when Clara stood before her she said, "From now on, Clara, don't let anyone into the house when I am gone."

"What is it, Frau Platt?" Clara asked, wringing her hands.

"He said my husband owed him money, and I had to give it to him. He would have gone to the police."

Clara shook her head. "He told me he was your friend! How sorry I am, how sorry!"

"You couldn't have known," Mother sighed. "It's times like these that prove what people really are. Well, let's have supper. I feel exhausted." She coughed, pressing a handkerchief to her lips. "It's this cold," she murmured, "that's making me tired. I should see Dr. Michels. Ah, there is so much to do. At least we have our passports. That's the main thing."

"Oh, there's a letter," Clara said, "from Herr Platt. It came while you were gone."

Instantly Mother's face brightened, and Annie cried, "Read it! What does he tell me? Read it!"

Annie climbed up into Mother's lap, and Ruth and I stood close beside her to see Papa's handwriting while she read.

My dear wife and daughters,

My thoughts are with you constantly, and I hope you have made plans for your holiday in Switzerland. Annie, be a good girl and stay very close to your mother on the trip.

I have found a place in a rooming house where the landlady speaks German. The woman is a good soul, and reminds me somewhat of our Clara, although, of course, her cooking cannot compare.

We all looked at Clara, and she smiled self-consciously.

At night I go to school to learn English. My girls, you would laugh to see me sitting behind a desk like a young schoolboy!

My very dear friend has a job selling neckties. He also works in the mornings, sweeping and dusting in one of the large office buildings. In the afternoons he goes to the garment district to sell his neckties and to talk with men in the clothing business. He is hoping to go into the coat business here someday.

All my love,

Papa

"What does he mean?" I whispered. "His very dear friend?"

Mother shook her head slightly, then glanced at Clara.

"Come on, Annie," Clara said. "Help me take those cookies off the pans."

When the kitchen door had closed behind them, Mother said, "Do be careful what you say around

Annie, Lisa. Papa means, of course, that *he* has a job selling neckties—and sweeping. He's just being cautious. If people should find out he is working in America, they would know he doesn't intend to come back, and it could be—well—awkward for us. Now, we don't have to tell Grandmother Platt what sort of work Papa is doing. You know how she is."

"He's a janitor," Ruth said, wide-eyed.

"Yes," Mother replied sternly, "and probably the best janitor they ever had."

I kept silent, but somehow, I, too, had imagined that in America Papa would be making and selling coats, as he had always done. I had heard that in America everybody was rich. I could not picture my father, whose shirts were always spotlessly white and whose shoes were polished until they gleamed, being a janitor, perhaps in overalls. It was too absurd, my Papa! *He's doing it for us,* I thought, overcome with love, and longing to see him.

THE SACRIFICE

ON THE LAST DAY WE WOULD BE IN school, I gave Rosemarie a snapshot of myself. The day after next we were leaving.

"It's a good picture of you, Lisa," Rosemarie said.

"It shows all my freckles," I objected.

"I think freckles are interesting," Rosemarie said seriously. "Really, I think they add character to a face. Your hair is really nice here too. You know," she said, looking at me closely, "I think it is getting a little more red in it."

I laughed. "Remember the time I put lemon juice on it? Then vinegar? I smelled like a tossed salad."

"Yes. Remember that book we read? What did it say? 'Her hair was like sparks'?"

I quoted, having memorized the passage. "In the sunlight her hair shone with dazzling red lights, like sparks from a firecracker.'" We had read the book together in Rosemarie's room, until her sister caught us and took it away.

"Remember the afternoon we went ice skating, and your beads broke and spilled all over the ice?"

"Remember the day we took Annie to the park, and we couldn't get her down out of that tree?"

We spent the afternoon together, remembering, and I am sure that Rosemarie knew I wasn't coming back.

"Write to me, Lisa," she begged, and I promised I would. Then she unfastened her silver bracelet with the cloverleaf charm on which her name was engraved. "I want you to take this," she said, "to remember me by."

"But it has your name on it," I objected, "and you've always loved it."

"That's why I want you to wear it," Rosemarie insisted.

"Is it all right with your mother?"

"Of course," Rosemarie said firmly. "Please take it. Look, you can give it back if you want to—when I see you again."

"But, Rosemarie . . ." I stammered. I had never kept any secrets from her before. "Are you planning," I hesitated, "to take a—a vacation too?"

Rosemarie shook her head. "I don't think so. My father doesn't want to leave his patients. You know how it is."

I knew how many people needed Rosemarie's father, Dr. Michels. He was our family doctor too. Now, more than ever, his office would be filled with patients; for Jewish people could go only to Jewish doctors. And Dr. Michels was staying here, facing whatever dangers would come, for his first duty was always to the sick. My thoughts were jumbled, and I felt a heaviness in my chest. I couldn't help thinking of what Clara had said about Papa, that it took courage for him to leave Germany. For Dr. Michels, the courageous thing was to remain. How strange it was, how difficult to understand, that Rosemarie's father and mine must do exactly the opposite, and that in each case it was right.

"All this will blow over," Rosemarie said with a smile and a wave of her hand. "You'll be back sooner than you think."

She gave me a quick kiss. "Have a good trip, Lisa."

The next afternoon we said good-bye to the family. They came, one after the other, uncles, aunts, cousins, grandparents, all saying, "What a commotion! We ought to leave you alone so you can pack." They spoke only of pleasant things, as if we were truly going on a pleasure trip.

Tante Helga, my beautiful young aunt, held me tight, then said with a faint smile, "Just don't forget your native language, darling. Someday I will come to America to see you, and oh, what grand times we will have. You'll teach me to speak English then, won't you? And you'll show me the sights. But remember your German, too. It will always help you to know another language."

I loved Tante Helga more than any of the other aunts. Perhaps it was because she had no children of her own that we were so close. For some reason, of all her nieces and nephews, Tante Helga had always chosen me when it came to going places like the Children's Ballet or to puppet shows. At Christmastime she always took me to the big department stores to see the decorations, and she and I selected gifts for the whole family together.

"I'll miss you, Tante Helga," I said softly, kissing her cheek.

"Oh no," she said. "Not you. You'll be so busy storing up new information. You always collect new ideas," she said, laughing, "like a squirrel gathering nuts for winter."

We said good-bye to one after the other of our relatives. They left hastily, so that there would be no time for tears. But even so my grandmother cried terribly. She clung to Mother's hands, and the lines in her face were deep and pitiful. "Margo, my child," she wept, "when in this life will we ever meet again?"

"I'll send for you, Mama," my mother told her again and again. "I'll send for you, I promise."

At last our suitcases were packed, ready for the morning. There was only one for each of us.

"Can't we take just one more suitcase?" I begged Mother.

"No," she answered. "We're taking only what we would need on a short vacation."

There were so many things I couldn't bear to leave—ballet costumes, books, school albums.

"You'll each wear a sweater and carry a coat," Mother said. "We have to save room in the suitcases."

"I would be taking my violin on a vacation trip," Ruth said.

Mother paused for a moment, then nodded. "Very well, Ruth, you may carry your violin."

"Frau Platt, what about the silver?" Clara asked, carrying a tray of silverware. "Couldn't you put some of this in among your clothes?"

"Of course not," Mother replied. "They will be inspecting our luggage at the border." She chuckled. "Do people bring their own silverware on a vacation?"

"But all these things!" Clara exclaimed. "Your books, the paintings, the linens . . ."

"Take whatever you can carry, Clara," Mother said. "Take it home with you after we are gone, and use it."

"I couldn't!"

"I want you to have it," Mother told her. "The Nazis will take what is left. You know that."

"I won't use it," Clara said, wringing her hands. "I'll take home what I can and keep it for you."

"Let's talk downstairs, Clara," Mother said. "Lisa, Ruth, it's time for bed. We're leaving very early in the morning."

"Try to leave Germany," I heard Mother tell Clara.

"I can't, Frau Platt. My mother . . . ," Clara replied.

"Take your mother and leave as soon as you can. Go to England or France. There's going to be a war."

The door closed and I could hear no more. I began to walk through the rooms, looking at everything we would leave behind the next morning, but still I could not actually believe that war was coming. War was something distant and strange that happened to other people in other times. I had read of wars, of wounded men, of fleeing women and children and of death. I had heard of women ripping up sheets into bandages, of people searching for coal and for food, and even of people eating their pets in times of great hunger.

Mauschen! My mouth went dry with terror. My beautiful cat! What would become of him? Who would remember to feed him and call him in at night? Who would protect him if there were great hunger?

I ran into the kitchen. "Clara! Clara!" I burst out. "Will you take Mauschen home with you? He'll cry so when we leave. Please, don't let a stranger get him. They might—sometimes in a war . . ." I couldn't say it or even think of it, my little Mauschen, a little brown fuzzy kitten when I first got him.

"Lischen! Be calm. Of course I will take him," Clara said, coming to put her arms around me. "I won't let him go to any stranger."

I rushed to the back porch where Mauschen slept in his little basket. I had named him that because he looked so like a little mouse at first, but now he was sleek and beautiful. I picked him up and held him close, and he gave a soft, sleepy meow.

Clara took him from my arms. "He's a beautiful cat," she murmured, "a sweet cat. I'll take care of him always, I promise."

"And take his basket, too," I said. "He's used to it."

"I will," Clara said, kissing me. "Now go to bed, and don't worry. Sleep well, Lischen."

"Good night, Clara." I turned back, for I had seen a long salami, still in its wrapper, lying on the counter. "Can I have that?" I asked.

"The salami?" Clara asked, bewildered. "You don't even like salami."

Still, I wanted it.

"Well, all right, take it," Clara said, shaking her head in confusion. Then her expression changed to one of deep tenderness. "Of course. I understand. Take it with you, my child."

In my room I put the salami in the bottom of my suitcase, concealing it from Ruth, who would have laughed at me and called me a silly goose. "One salami won't keep you from starving," she would have taunted, but somehow it made me feel better to have it.

I lay down on my bed, feeling too tired to move a muscle. All day I had packed, choosing the few things I could take with me. Then I had cleaned and dusted everything, books, ice skates, games, my doll collection, taking each thing into my hands. Ruth couldn't understand why I was cleaning everything when it had to be left behind anyway, and I couldn't explain it. I just needed to have everything in order.

Ruth was still rummaging through her things. "Aren't you finished yet?" I yawned deeply. "Let's go to bed."

"I'm almost ready," she mumbled, bending over her violin case.

I sat up suddenly, realizing that Ruth was slipping something under the lining of her violin case.

"What are you doing?" I cried.

"Never mind," Ruth said.

"Ruth!" It was money that she was hiding so carefully. "You can't do that!" I exclaimed.

"Nobody will look here," Ruth said, still working. "You heard Mother say that we can only take ten marks apiece. Anybody can see that won't be enough to last until we get to America."

"That's smuggling," I gasped. "Don't you know what happened to the Mullers?"

"Shut up," Ruth said fiercely. "Stop yelling. You don't have to know anything about this. It's my money, my birthday money."

I watched as she laid the bills flat against the side of the case, took a tube of glue and applied it to the loose material of the lining, then pressed it down firmly against the case.

"Look now," she said. "Nothing shows."

I went over to see. "Don't do it," I begged. "It isn't right."

"Don't be so stupid," she retorted. "We have to help ourselves any way we can. I've been planning this all along."

"I'll tell Mother," I threatened.

"If you dare!" Ruth stepped toward me, clenching her fist. "If you dare!" Then her tone changed. "Look," she coaxed, "Mother will be so happy when I give her this money in Switzerland. She'll need it for food. Can you imagine what it's like to be hungry? I mean really hungry, with nothing at all to eat. Think of Annie, crying for food. Mother's got enough to worry about. Papa even said we have to take responsibility."

"Look at this," I said, pointing to a damp spot on the lining.

"It will be dry by morning," Ruth said confidently. "You'll be glad I did this. You'll see. Look, it's good as new. Nothing shows."

I yawned again. It was impossible to win an argument with Ruth, and I was very tired. "It's all right," I sighed. "Just come to bed."

I must have fallen asleep in a moment. Suddenly I sat up with a start. Under the door I saw a faint light, and then I heard a thump and a soft cry. I slipped out of bed and tiptoed across the hall to Annie's room.

She was standing over a large carton holding several dolls in her arms. I heard a sniff and then I saw that she was crying, and she mumbled to herself, "I won't leave you. I'll take you all with me."

"Annie! What in the world are you doing?" I whispered. "You're supposed to be asleep."

"I'm packing," Annie answered without looking at me.

"But Mother's already packed your things. You can't take all those dolls."

"I'm not leaving them," Annie said with a stubborn nod.

"Now, Annie, listen to me. Please stop a minute and listen." I knelt down beside her, and Annie clung to me. Her face was hot and damp, and the short dark curls stood out all over her head. I kissed her cheeks and held her. "Don't cry, Baby, don't cry. Sit down here." I pulled her up on the bed beside me. "Let's talk about it."

"I don't want to talk," Annie mumbled. "I'm not going to leave my Susans here alone."

All of Annie's dolls were named Susan. We teased her about it, but she was determined to give all of them her favorite name.

"They won't be alone," I whispered. "They'll

have each other, and when we come back . . ."

"You know we're not coming back!" she said in a voice filled with reproach.

"Annie!"

"I've heard you all talking. We're never coming back. We're going to America."

"Hush!" I said. "You mustn't say that, not to anybody. You're not supposed to know. Do you understand?" I had grasped Annie's arm too tightly, and she began to cry.

"Shh," I tried to silence her. "Mother will hear you. Now look at me and listen, because this is very important." Her large, dark eyes were frightened. "If anybody asks you where we are going, you must say that we're going to Switzerland for a vacation. Now say that."

"Switzerland," Annie mumbled.

"For a vacation," I added, still holding her beneath the chin, firmly.

"For a vacation," Annie repeated, struggling slightly, "and I'm taking all my dolls with me."

"You are *not*. We don't have room." Annie's lip began to quiver again.

"Don't cry!" I warned her. "Now, Mother said you can take two dolls, and that's all." I took a deep breath, struggling for patience. "Let's decide which ones."

We took the dolls out of the carton and laid them on the bed.

"Which one first?" I asked Annie, knowing what she would say.

"The baby doll," Annie replied, clutching the torn stuffed doll to her chest. "She needs a mommy the most, because she's always coming apart."

"All right, then you'll take her. Now one more."

Annie walked back and forth, biting her lip in concentration. She touched each doll, fingered their dresses, and finally sighed. "I can't decide. I'll have to take them all."

I shook my head, knowing there was only one thing to do. It had been in my mind from the beginning.

SONIA LEVITIN

"You like my bride doll, don't you?" I asked her.

Annie's eyes were wide and she gasped, "Your bride doll! She's the most beautiful doll in the world!"

Aunt Helga had given me the bride doll for my last birthday. "A twelve-year-old girl is really too old to play with dolls," she had said, "but every girl should have a last doll, a very special doll to keep her company while she is growing up." The doll was beautiful, eight inches tall, with a white dress and veil of handmade lace. She wore a tiny pearl necklace and white high-heeled shoes.

I closed my eyes for a moment, picturing the little bride doll. I had packed it carefully this afternoon.

"If you promise," I told Annie slowly, "not to say a single word about America, not to anybody, I'll let you have my bride doll."

Annie gasped. "For keeps?"

"Yes."

"I promise! I promise!" Annie cried, hopping up and down.

"If you break your promise," I told her in my sternest voice, "I'll take the doll away from you, and you'll never even be able to touch her again."

"I won't say a word," Annie whispered, her eyes shining.

"Now go to bed. Tomorrow morning—no, I'll get her now."

When I brought the doll, Annie immediately tucked it into bed beside her, crushing the lace dress under her covers. She put her thumb in her mouth and smiled at me, a crooked, blissful smile.

Very early the next morning, when we were almost ready to leave, Annie sat quietly on the sofa, dressed for the journey, holding her baby doll in one arm and the bride doll in the other.

"Lisa," Mother called. "Did you know Annie has your bride doll? Weren't you going to pack it?"

"I gave it to Annie," I said, avoiding Mother's eyes. "I'm getting too old to play with dolls."

THE LAST
BARRIER

IT WAS BARELY DAYBREAK. THE NEIGHBORS
still slept. Their houses were dark and silent. I turned
for a moment to look back at the house where I had
lived almost all my life, at the small courtyard where
I used to play with my dolls, at the low wrought-
iron gate, at the upstairs window of my bedroom and
the white lacy curtains Clara had made. I glanced at
the lilies that grew by the walk. I had planted them
myself only a year before.

The taxi was waiting, and Clara, with her apron on,
came with us to the waiting car. "Good-bye," she said
loudly, just in case someone should be awake to hear,

"have a good vacation. I'll see you in a few weeks."
She reached into her pocket. "Here's something for
you to have on the train." She gave each of us a small
round tin of candies.

I put my arms around Clara. "Thank you, Clara."
There was so much I wanted to say to her, but my
voice broke at the word: "Good-bye."

"Don't cry, Lischen," she said, but her eyes, too,
were full.

"Come, Lisa," Mother called me. "Help Annie
into the taxi. We have to hurry. The train leaves in
an hour."

The taxi sped down the street with the driver
whistling softly to himself. I had never seen the city
at dawn before. The streets were hushed and shad-
owy, with only a few merchants moving about, preparing for the day.

We drove past the big park, where we had spent
many afternoons playing with friends and wander-
ing along the paths of the zoo. The bandstand was

deserted, the swings hung limp and silent. Later children would come to play while their mothers had coffee and cake on the terrace overlooking the playground, and nursemaids in white dresses would wheel fine baby carriages along the tree-lined paths.

I felt a tightness in my throat. *Surely,* I thought, *surely it would always be this way.* On every Sunday afternoon, long after we were gone, the band would play Viennese waltzes and boys would play ball on the lawn, and children would beg to ride the carousel. Families like ours would meet their friends and sit around the tables, laughing and talking.

How could it ever be different?

But already things were different. It had been a slow, gradual change, like a shadow crossing the sun, bringing a strange cold feeling that one could not quite explain.

At first it had been a curious sight to see men in uniform with their armbands and high black boots. Little children would stand at a distance, staring and whispering. But soon even Annie knew that those men must be avoided.

Every day on the way to school Ruth and I saw the soldiers, their arms linked as they strode through the streets, laughing and singing loudly. It was the students, though, with their brown shirts and black ties bearing the swastika emblem, who were the worst. They pushed their way through the busy streets, walking five and six abreast, as if they owned the city. They sang new songs, and one in particular was so horrible that I could not believe my ears.

When the blood of Jews spurts from our knives,
Then things will be twice as good as before!

On the street corners there were soldiers shaking their collection boxes, shouting in chorus, "Give, give, give to the Nazi party!" Every time I saw them I wanted to run, and the sound of those jangling coins pounded in my ears, but Ruth and I would walk past, keeping our faces blank.

Then one afternoon we had been forced to stop. We had been out shopping with Mother, and suddenly we could walk no farther. The street was roped off, and swarms of people had gathered.

"There's going to be a parade," Mother had said, her face ashen. "Oh, children, if I had known! We'll have to stand here until it's over." She grasped Annie's hand tightly and said in her sternest voice, "Don't move, Annie, and don't you dare cry!"

All I could see through the crowd were the tops of helmets and black marching feet. Drums thundered; horns and trumpets made a deafening blast. Flags waved everywhere, not the German flag we loved, but the bright red Nazi flag with the black hooked cross.

Suddenly a tremendous roar came from the crowd. "Heil Hitler! Heil Hitler!" The whole street seemed to vibrate with it, "Heil Hitler!" and I trembled and wondered whether my legs would hold me upright. It seemed that we were the only people who did not join the shouting. We had stood motionless, surrounded by the roaring crowd, until finally it was over. We went home, but things were never quite the same again. Now the taxi slammed to an abrupt halt, and Annie nearly fell off the seat.

"What's the matter, driver?" Mother asked, frowning.

"Can't get through here," the driver muttered. "They're preparing for a rally and a parade."

"A parade at this time of the morning?" Mother exclaimed.

"See that poster? It's not starting until ten, but they're blocking off the street and setting up a platform for speakers."

From the window I could see soldiers inspecting the grounds. Some were hanging a huge Nazi flag behind the platform.

"Oh," Annie piped up with a little giggle, "how beautiful."

I wanted to pinch her.

"Herr Hitler himself will speak today," said the taxi driver proudly. "Too bad you have to miss it."

"Yes," Mother said faintly, and now I gave Annie a fierce look and nodded toward the bride doll.

A guard with a black pistol in his belt came over to the car. "You can't get through here," he said gruffly. "No cars allowed until after the parade."

The taxi driver yawned and scratched his head. "Guess I'll turn around and take the next street."

"You can't. It's barricaded too. You'll have to turn there." The guard pointed. "Where are you headed?"

"The railroad station."

"Then you'll have to go up about six blocks, then left. . . ."

I saw Mother looking at her watch, shaking her head. Then she reached into her purse and suddenly got out of the taxi and walked up to the guard.

"How silly of me to forget about the parade today," I heard her say in a gay voice. "It's a shame. I know the children would love to see it." She smiled brightly.

"If you can wait," said the guard, "I could arrange to save some chairs for you and your children. Think what it would mean to them to see the Führer so close!" His eyes gleamed.

"You are very kind," Mother said. "Unfortunately, we have relatives meeting us in Switzerland at the station. It's the only train today. I suppose the children will get over their disappointment. I told my girls that of course you couldn't move the barricade just for us."

The guard glanced over his shoulder. "I suppose they can see another parade soon," he said, "and they are probably excited about this trip."

He glanced inside the taxi. Annie's face was pressed against the window, and she waved and smiled happily.

Mother held out her hand. Between her fingers was a folded and crumpled bill.

"I suppose I could let you through," he mused.

"You are very kind to take the trouble," Mother said.

"Not at all," he replied, taking the bill and putting it into his pocket. "I wouldn't want you to miss your train. I know how children look forward to these things—I have two of my own."

"Nice fellow," said the driver when the barricade had been moved and we continued along the street toward the station.

We had barely boarded the train before the engines began to hiss and puff and we were moving. Mother asked the porter to turn one of the seats around, so that we could all face each other. Then she leaned back, her eyes closed. Her face looked very white, and I wondered whether she had slept at all the night before.

Suddenly she sat up, coughing, and pointed to the water fountain at the end of the car.

Ruth ran to bring water in a paper cup. "You never did see Dr. Michels," she said.

"I know," Mother sighed. "There was so much to

do. I'll be all right. Just let me rest awhile. You can tell Annie some stories."

"Come sit between us," Ruth said to Annie, and she began to tell Annie her favorite story, "Cinderella."

Mother leaned toward us suddenly and whispered, "Listen, I forgot to tell you. At the border they might ask us whether we have any valuables. If they say you cannot take your rings, you'll have to give them up. Do you understand?"

Ruth and I nodded, but I really did not understand, and I looked down at my beautiful ring and watched the light from the window shining through the stone.

It was a strange, long morning. I had brought a book to read, but I couldn't concentrate on anything except the click of the wheels and the sound of the engine.

I saw a little boy sitting on a fence, waving frantically as the train sped by, but I did not wave back.

Ruth came close beside me to look out the window. "We'll never come back," she whispered.

"Maybe—someday." I said.

Never, never, my thoughts repeated in rhythm to the clicking wheels. The train followed the course of the Rhine River—Frankfurt, where we went for winter vacation, Heidelberg, with the large old stone castle on the hill—all the places we had loved.

At last the train lurched and came to a stop. There was a great deal of grumbling. "Why are we stopping here?" a woman exclaimed crossly. "This stop isn't scheduled."

"Last stop before the border," the conductor shouted, passing through our car.

After a few minutes a man in uniform came onto the train. I recognized the black armband and the high black boots.

"Jews out!" he shouted. "Jews out for inspection."

I stared at Mother, unable to speak.

"What a bother," someone complained. "We'll all be delayed."

"Jews out!" the Nazi shouted again. "Out!" He looked around the car.

"Come on, girls," Mother said in a low voice.

My hands were moist, and my face felt hot. I would never be able to walk through that train. I shook my head blindly, wanting to scream, but the words came out in a whisper, "I can't."

"We must!" Mother took my arm. "You must obey, Lisa! Come, don't be afraid."

"Bring all your belongings," said the officer when he saw us standing.

"Take your coat, Lisa," Mother said, "and your violin, Ruth."

Ruth took the violin from under her seat, and I felt Mother pulling me toward the aisle. "Lisa, *please*," she whispered.

Numbly I began to walk. Everyone's head was turned toward us. We were the only ones in the car who had to leave. With every step I took the aisle seemed to stretch out longer, but I put one foot in front of the other and kept my eyes straight ahead.

But they were staring at us, all those eyes, and I wanted to scream at all of them, "Why do you look at us? We're no different than anyone else!" Dimly I saw Annie scampering ahead of me, then she turned and I saw her smiling, and I thought of the Mullers.

All the suitcases were piled at the end of the car. Mother began to search for ours. She told Ruth and me to carry our own, and then a man with gray hair came up to us.

"Allow me to help you," he said softly, taking a suitcase in each hand.

"Thank you," Mother murmured.

"It's beyond belief," he muttered under his breath.

Mother shook her head at him slightly, for the Nazi strode past us, calling, "Quick! Quick!"

We were led into a small wooden shack with a few

splintery benches along the walls and a large counter where another Nazi waited.

"Open the suitcases," he commanded.

With both hands he rummaged through my dresses, my underwear and pajamas, holding them up. He put his hand inside my shoes, then reached down to the bottom of the suitcase and took out the salami. His lips were pressed tightly together as he held up the salami. "Well? Don't you know that food is forbidden?" he shouted.

"This child," Mother said, coughing slightly, "simply loves salami."

I heard the salami land in the waste can behind the counter. My clothes were pushed back inside the suitcase.

When all four bags were closed once more, the man turned to Mother. "Have you any jewels?" he asked.

"Only what I am wearing," Mother said, showing her watch, necklace, and rings.

"You can tell me," he said with a forced smile. "You won't be punished. Surely you own more jewelry than that!"

"I have taken only what is allowed," Mother insisted.

"We'll see," he said sharply. "Frau Krantz will make the personal inspection. This way."

She was a round-faced woman with braids wound around her head, wearing a dark blue uniform. "Remove your shoes and outer clothing," she said to Mother, when we were in the small, cold room. Ruth and Annie and I sat down on the bench, watching while the woman quickly searched through Mother's shoes, the pockets of her dress, the lining of her coat. Then she said, "Take everything out of your purse and put it on the table."

My flesh felt cold at the thought that this woman would touch me, examine me down to my skin as if I were a criminal.

"Now the children," she said. She hesitated. "The children need only take off their shoes and coats."

She put her hands inside my shoes and felt the folds of my dress and coat, then she looked at my ring, but said nothing. She opened the door and called out, "These people have nothing."

We stepped outside the shack into the sunlight, and again we saw the Nazi who had come onto the train. He held up his hand to stop us, then knelt down beside Annie.

"What a pretty doll you have," he said. "May I see her?"

Annie stared at him woodenly and clutched the bride doll more tightly against her chest.

"Show the officer your doll, Annie," Mother said.

Annie held the doll toward him, biting her lip as he searched through the dress and veil.

"Very well," he said, turning with a brisk click of his heels. "You may—wait! I see we have missed something. What is that?" he asked, pointing at Ruth's violin case.

"It's my violin," Ruth said in a whisper.

"It is forbidden to take musical instruments," he declared.

"But I only—I have to practice."

"Musical instruments are strictly *forbidden*!"

"Give it up, Ruth," Mother said in a low, urgent voice. "Give it!"

We walked back to the train, Ruth with her head down. I looked back for a moment and saw that he had taken the violin from its case and was stroking the smooth wood with his fingertips. Ruth did not notice, and all the way to Zurich she did not speak.

ZURICH—
CITY OF REFUGE

IT WAS LATE AT NIGHT WHEN WE REACHED
Zurich. At the railroad station, while Mother went to
get a newspaper, Annie fell asleep with her head on a
suitcase, and we could scarcely wake her to board the
bus that would take us to the rooming house.

"I had hoped to rent an apartment," Mother
sighed, "but everything is so expensive."

I could see the shining water of Zurich Lake as
the bus traveled on, and behind it the hills, dotted
with houses whose lights sent their reflection down
to the lake. It was beautiful, almost unreal, like a picture postcard.

At the rooming house we climbed the sagging stairway two flights, followed by Frau Feldin, the landlady. She was very thin, and she reminded me of a bird, talking incessantly in a high, chirping voice.

"I hope your little girl doesn't wet," she said rapidly to Mother. "I don't have many sheets, you know, and you'll have to launder your own."

"Oh, Annie doesn't wet anymore," Mother replied. "She's nearly four."

"We have so many boarders now," Frau Feldin said, her hands fluttering. "We used to have only one man living with us, but times change, so many refugees now. You have one of the biggest rooms," she said, "with a stove and an icebox. The bathroom is down the hall. I'll leave you now. If you need anything…" Her voice trailed off, and from the stairway she called, *"Grüss Gott,"* the Swiss phrase for greeting and parting, "God greet you."

The room had the musty odor of old, faded things, and I wondered, if this was one of the largest rooms, what the small ones were like.

"Where shall we put our things?" Ruth asked.

"Here." Mother pointed to a dark, heavy cupboard. "But wait until tomorrow to unpack."

I walked to the window and looked to the alley below, where garbage pails and old crates were the only view. The drapes on the window and across the tiny kitchen nook were heavy with soil and unevenly faded, the yellow and green patterns of ferns blending together.

"Let's go to bed," Mother said cheerfully, "and tomorrow we'll get acquainted with the city. Maybe we'll even find a larger room."

I felt vaguely hungry, but was too tired even to mention it, and I knew the cupboards were empty. Annie was put to bed on the sofa, while Ruth and I slept in the double bed beside Mother's cot. The sheets felt slightly damp, but after lying for a few moments in the darkness I fell asleep. Then, from far, far away it seemed, I saw a light and heard Mother's voice, "Oh, Annie, my darling, you did wet the bed, and I told the landlady . . ." But I was too tired to stay awake.

In the morning we took our first walk around the city, and in the days that followed Ruth and I became familiar with the streets and shops, for there was not much else to do. The children, free from school for summer vacation, were swimming in Zurich Lake and going in sailboats and motorboats, but this was not for us. Entrance to the lakeside beach cost money, and we could not spend the little that was left in Mother's purse.

There was no larger room to be had, nor any room that would not cost nearly twice as much as Frau Feldin's. "We'll manage," Mother said when Ruth complained of the cramped quarters. "It probably won't be for long." But with Papa's next letters we began to realize that we might have to stay in Zurich for several months.

"There is a great deal involved," Papa wrote. "I must save enough money for your tickets, then find a sponsor for you. It will probably be several months, but remember that I am doing all I can."

I had not seen Papa for five months. Why should it take so long simply to go to another country? Mother said that Papa had to find witnesses who would swear that he could support us. There were forms to fill out, and each form meant that we had to wait a little longer. And there were thousands like us, people from all over the world, trying to get to America. It would take time, and everyone was fighting against time, trying to settle somewhere in safety before war overtook them.

People from Austria, Poland, Lithuania, and Czechoslovakia had gathered a few possessions as we had done, and become refugees. I hated that word.

"There is an agency to help refugees," Frau Feldin told Mother. "I've heard that they sometimes find homes for refugee children. It is too crowded, the four of you in that room."

"I'll keep the children with me," Mother said. "I want us to stay together," and she added softly, "as long as possible."

Night after night, when Ruth and I were in bed, I saw Mother sitting at the table counting the money that was left. She scarcely ate, taking only a cup of tea for breakfast, while she gave us slices of bread and butter. And then one day I saw that Mother's diamond engagement ring was gone, and I asked her, knowing the answer beforehand, "What happened to your ring?"

"I sold it."

There was nothing left of value now, except for Ruth's ring and mine.

"Maybe we should sell them," I said to Ruth one day when we were out walking. Day after day we walked and looked at the shop windows filled with beautiful, tempting displays of toys, watches, pretty clothes, and music boxes. I had never cared that much for owning things, but now, without a penny in my pocket, all I could think of was going in to buy something, anything. The bakery shop, with its little cakes all arranged and the wonderful sweet smells made me think of home, where the cookie jar was always full and the aroma of Clara's baking filled the house.

We hurried past the bakery, and in the next window we saw an odd assortment of gold watches, dishes, furniture, and clothing.

"It's a pawnshop," Ruth told me.

"I know."

"Maybe we should . . ."

"Do you think so?"

"Papa said we should sell them when we needed money."

Before I could answer Ruth had stepped inside, and the little bell tinkled as I followed her into the small, dim shop.

We stood at the cluttered counter until the man, wearing thick glasses, approached us. "Yes?"

Ruth held out her hand. "I want to sell my ring," she said resolutely. "How much will you give me?"

"I'd have to look at it closely," he said, smiling as if someone had made a joke.

His expression changed to one of astonishment when he examined the ring under his glass. He came toward us, shaking his head and saying soberly, "I cannot buy this. This is a real stone. You would have to have your mother's permission."

Ruth's cheeks were flushed. "It's *my* ring," she said.

"I'm sorry, Fraulein," he replied. "If your mother agrees that you should sell it, I'll be glad to talk to her about it."

Outside, Ruth's face was still rigid with anger, and when I stumbled into a puddle, she lashed out at me, "Now look what you've done! You'll ruin your shoes. Why can't you be careful?"

I didn't answer, and she went on, nearly in tears, "If only he hadn't taken my violin!"

"I know," I whispered, taking Ruth's hand briefly. Then, as we walked past another toy shop, I suddenly remembered. Tomorrow was Annie's birthday, and we had nothing to give her.

"Of course I remembered Annie's birthday," Mother

said later when I mentioned it. "And we'll do something special. We'll all go to the park, and maybe we can take a ride on the funicular up to the Uetliberg. Frau Feldin says the view from the top of the mountain is wonderful, and it's a thrilling ride."

"I'll go tell Annie," I said, but Mother stopped me.

"No, let's surprise her."

"You think we might not be able to go," I said. "It costs money, doesn't it?"

"It does," Mother said rather sharply, "but I'm going to manage it. Tomorrow morning we're going to the agency. They will help us," she said confidently, but the look of concern she wore so often was still there.

I saw that same look on nearly every face when we sat waiting at the agency office the next day. We were lucky to have found seats on a wooden bench, for the room was filled with people, some leaning against the walls, little children sitting on the floor, all in a hot, humid room filled with the sound of typewriters, the ringing of telephones, and the low, constant babble of voices speaking in foreign languages.

After nearly two hours of waiting, our turn came at last, and we were led into a small room cluttered with books and papers.

A woman with bright yellow hair and dark-rimmed glasses looked up at us from behind her desk.

"May I have your name, please?" She was ready to begin writing.

"Margo Platt," said Mother, "and my three daughters. We are here from Germany to join my husband in—"

"Wait until I ask you. I must fill out the form."

The woman wrote rapidly, while Mother sat down and we stood beside her.

"Ages of your children?" Her voice tapped out the words like a machine. "Husband's occupation? Present address?"

Finally the woman stopped writing and looked up at Mother.

"Did you leave Germany by your own choice?" she asked, blinking rapidly.

"Yes, of course," Mother replied. "You know how things are for us there."

"What is your problem, Frau Platt?"

"I have hardly any money left. We were allowed to take out only ten marks apiece."

"Have you family in Germany?"

"Yes—my mother, my husband's brothers. But you know they can't send any money out."

"Wouldn't they help you if you were in Germany?" She fixed her eyes keenly on Mother, then glanced briefly at us, and by her look I felt that surely my hair was untidy, and that maybe I had forgotten to wash my face.

"If we were in Germany," Mother said, breathing heavily, "we wouldn't need their help." She spoke slowly, distinctly, as if somehow this woman was unable to follow the point of the conversation. "We left all our money and all our possessions in Germany," Mother explained. "I was told that this agency would help me."

"Of course, there are funds for certain cases," the woman said, still looking at Mother intently, "but you left Germany by your own choice. You were not driven out."

"Not driven out!" Mother repeated.

"Many Jewish people are still living in Germany, and without harm."

Mother's eyes were wide, and I saw the tight grip of her fingers on the arms of the chair. "Don't you know what is going on? Don't you read the newspapers, the arrests, the beatings . . ."

"Frau Platt," she said as if she were reasoning patiently with a stubborn child, "I would suggest very seriously that you take your children back to Germany. You have no way to support yourself here. Since you left Germany by your own choice, there is nothing we can do for you."

Mother's knuckles were white from her grip. "I am not going back," she said with soft fury, her eyes narrowing. "I'll never go back to Germany. We have come this far, and we will stay, even if you will not help. Come, girls!"

Mother swept out of the office so quickly that Annie had to run to keep up, and she panted, "Where are we going, Mama? Where?"

"To the park," Mother said, her voice strangely high-pitched. "To the park," she repeated, pulling Annie along beside her, while Ruth and I rushed to follow, not daring to speak.

Mother sat down on the park bench and told us, still in that strange, high tone, "Go and play, girls. Leave me. I have to think."

I didn't want to walk away from Mother, even for a moment, but I went with Annie and Ruth to the swings. We pushed Annie higher and higher, until she giggled and squealed, and then we took her to play in the sandbox.

"We'll have to sell our rings now," I told Ruth softly.

"Mother probably won't let us," she replied. "I asked

her last night. She said we have to save something for a real emergency."

"And isn't this a real emergency?" I demanded, but Ruth only shrugged. "Maybe we could get a job," I said, "washing dishes or delivering things."

"You always think everything is so simple!" Ruth snapped. "People can't work in a country when they're just visiting. If it were that easy, Mother would get a job."

"What can we do, then?"

"Nothing."

Ruth left me abruptly and went to help Annie build a sand castle. All around me children were laughing and shouting and playing on the bars, but I felt all alone, and I sat down on the warm grass with my eyes closed, wishing, pretending, half praying, wanting to believe that the strength of my thoughts could reach out and make something happen, make somebody care.

I opened my eyes and swallowed hard. I had made a resolution. *They* wouldn't make me cry. But as I looked toward the benches at my mother I saw, or I knew by the tilt of her body, that she was crying.

I ran to her. "Mother!" I sat beside her, my arms around her. "Please don't cry, Mother. Don't be unhappy."

Mother tried to wipe the tears away. "I was so sure that the agency would help us," she said, shaking her head. "I just don't know where to turn."

"Should we write to Papa? Can't he help?"

"What help, child? Your father told me to go to the agency. If I only knew someone. If we had a friend or a relative."

"Ruth and I want to sell our rings," I said quickly. "We want to help."

"No. We must keep something. If you want to help, just sit here quietly and let me think."

I sat and looked all around at the trees and the lawns, past the playground and up to the hills. I thought of the psalm I had learned long ago. "I will lift up mine eyes unto the hills, from whence cometh my help ..."

Softly I said to Mother, "I will pray."

"Yes, child, do," she murmured.

I might have prayed that something good would happen, but I had been taught that prayer is not for making wishes, but to seek strength and to praise God. "I will lift up mine eyes . . ."

"Lisa!" Mother said slowly, grasping my hand. "Maybe there is a way. At least I can try. Why didn't I think of it before? I'll go to a rabbi. He would know how to help. Ruth! Annie! Come, we're going."

At the rooming house Mother made a hasty telephone call, then she told us to stay and wait for her in the room. "Maybe I'll have good news," she said with a faint light of hope in her eyes. "We'll have your birthday treat another day, Annie," Mother said, kissing her. "You're a big girl now, you understand."

"It's all right," Annie said gravely, and I thought how much she had grown in just a few months, until I saw her reach for her old, ragged blanket and rub it against her cheek.

NEW FACES

"YOU DON'T HAVE TO GO," MOTHER TOLD US, "unless you want to."

"We'll go," Ruth said quickly. She had nodded to me as soon as Mother mentioned the camp that the rabbi had suggested. It was just an hour outside Zurich, and we would be able to visit Mother and Annie sometimes.

"Do you want to go, Lisa?" Mother asked me, watching my face intently.

I didn't want to go at all to this camp for refugee children, even though Mother spoke of having playmates there and said it was a chance for us

★★ 89 ★★

to get away from our crowded little room.

"We'll go," I said. "It will be fun."

"No it won't," Annie shouted, bursting into tears. "I don't want you to go! I'll be all alone!"

"We'll come to visit you," I told her. "Maybe we'll come every week."

"Lisa, don't go!" Annie cried, flinging her arms around me. "Take me with you."

"It's just for older children," Mother tried to explain. "Someday you'll have a chance to go somewhere too. Lisa and Ruth would like to make new friends and see other places."

"Let Ruth go, then!" Annie cried.

"I *want* to go," I told Annie. "And somebody has to stay with Mother to keep her company."

"That's right," Mother said quickly. "Think how lonesome I'd be with all my girls gone. Now you'll be the one to help me cook, Annie, and we'll go to the park together where you can play with other children."

"I don't love them. I don't want them. I want Lisa!" Annie sobbed.

I picked her up and put her on the sofa bed. "Lie down," I told her, "and I'll tell you a story. I'll tell you 'Cinderella.'" This time when I told of the wicked stepmother, Annie began to sob again, and I hurried through to tell about the king's ball, the glass slipper, and the prince coming to take Cinderella with him to his castle, where they lived happily ever after.

"It's not true," Annie said drowsily. "Things like that don't really happen."

"Yes they do," I said firmly. "Good things happen all the time. Now go to sleep!"

I wanted Annie to believe in the fairy tale, just as I wanted to make myself more cheerful, as I had promised Papa I would be. I glanced at Mother and saw for the first time how thin she had become, how loosely her dress fitted over her body. She was darning our socks again, patching our pajamas, making do.

The rabbi had told Mother that he would speak to

the agency personally, that they must help us. But help would be slight; there simply wasn't enough money for everyone. Mother just couldn't afford to keep us with her, but I tried not to think of it that way.

"At least we'll be together," I whispered to Ruth, when we lay in bed. "We might each have been sent to a separate family."

"I wouldn't want to live with another family," Ruth whispered back. "I'd feel like a stepchild."

"I guess it will be nice at the camp," I said.

Ruth didn't answer. I realized how accustomed I had become to the little room. It was, in a way, home, and the thought of going to a strange place, sleeping in a strange bed, gave me a fluttering feeling in my stomach.

That feeling of dread was with me still in the morning when Mother took us to the agency office. This time we saw a different clerk, a pretty young woman who smiled and took Mother's hand and told Ruth and me that the cook from the camp would come to the agency to meet us. "He's a nice old man," she said. "He used to be chief cook at the Hofstaader Hotel in Vienna."

He came at last, limping slightly as if one leg pained him, but he was tall and stout and robust and wore a white shirt and white trousers. His head was completely bald, except for a few bristling white hairs along the back of his neck.

"What a sweet little one!" he exclaimed, seeing Annie, and he bent down close to her. He asked us our names, then nodded to Mother. "I'm Emil Wagner," he said, "but the children all call me Pop. I've almost forgotten my other name," he chuckled.

"Come along then," he said, taking up our suitcases. "Two more for dinner. It's a shame we can't take this little one too, but . . ." He seemed to have forgotten his train of thought. "Come along. We must hurry. There is supper to prepare. Ah, there was a time when supper was truly an event—fourteen main dishes to cook, hot rolls, pastries, glazed fruits.

SONIA LEVITIN

Everybody who was *anybody* came through those
doors at the Hofstaader Hotel—dukes, counts, even
princes, yes."

After we had said good-bye to Mother and Annie,
and Ruth and I climbed into the cab of the battered
old truck, Pop continued as if he had never left off
remembering. "Six cook's helpers in my charge," he
murmured, "and two underchefs. There will come a
time again. Yes, it will be so again."

We bumped along the streets through the city,
then up into the hills. The truck swayed so violently that I could hardly speak. Ruth and I looked
at each other, and suddenly we both began to laugh;
I'm not sure why. Maybe it was the sudden freedom
of a truck ride though the country. Maybe because,
inside, we were lonely. And for reasons of his own,
Pop laughed with us. At last he wiped his bald head
with a handkerchief and mopped his face, sighing,
"Ah, such memories!"

Ruth and I sat silent. The old man was, somehow,

transported into another time. At last Ruth asked him timidly, "How is it at the camp?"

"You will see," he replied. He did not speak the rest of the way, until after he had maneuvered the truck over a series of terrible ruts, he pointed past the trees to a small clearing. "There it is. We're home."

The air was sultry and heavy when we stepped out of the truck and hurried behind Pop, who carried our suitcases.

It occurred to me that travelers are always following their suitcases, always in fear that they will be lost or stolen. The suitcase is the last and only familiar thing.

But even as I hurried, I glanced about. There was only the one old wooden building, somebody's forsaken barn, perhaps, but all around it stood huge pine trees, and I could smell a deep scent of sap and pine needles, mingled with the dust from the road and the odor of earth that is damp even before the rains come.

I'm not certain what I expected. I had read *Jane Eyre*, and perhaps from this I dreaded an institution of any sort, and expected severe mistresses and hard little cots all in a row, with lists of rules posted on the walls, and children marching uniformly to lessons or gymnastics.

We walked through a large hallway, and in a room to one side, I could only make out dull brown shapes of furniture, the kind that people give away when it is long past use. On the other side was the dining room, with three long wooden tables, and again I had the feeling that this place must once have been a stable.

Pop put down our suitcases and pointed to a door. "Just knock," he said. "Frau Strom is inside." He disappeared through a swinging door that must have led to the kitchen.

"Who's Frau Strom?" I whispered to Ruth, and Ruth replied, also in a whisper, "Probably the director."

Ruth's knock sounded loud and bold, and I wanted

to crouch back into the shadows, but the door swung open. "Yes—yes, come in."

The voice sounded hurried, flustered, and as we entered Frau Strom gave us only a darting glance and continued to patter back and forth, plucking up an object here and there, searching aimlessly and with "tss-tss" sounds of despair. And it was no wonder that she couldn't find anything. I had never in my life seen such a mess, powder spilled on the dresser top, clothing draped over chairs, and every little space crammed with bottles and boxes and half-empty cups of tea.

She snatched her curling iron from the hot plate, which was beginning to give off a bitter smelling smoke, and, holding a bit of hair tightly between the hot iron, she turned to us.

"So you are the new girls." She looked back at the mirror, released a tight little curl, and gave it a pat. Her face was marked with ruddy places, from little blood vessels that had burst, and her eyes were never still, her tone a little breathless, as if she had been rushing all day.

"Did you bring sheets?" she asked.

I shook my head, and Ruth answered aloud, "No, we didn't. We don't have any."

"Same old story." She began another curl. "They said you would come at noon."

"We waited for the cook," Ruth explained.

"Now I'll have to make out a new list," Frau Strom said accusingly. "They want it alphabetical. *Why* does everything have to be alphabetical? What is your last name?"

"Platt," I said.

"Our mother is in Zurich," Ruth supplied, "and our father is in America."

"I'll show you your beds." She went to the door and motioned for us to follow.

We went up the stairs, and I wondered at the silence. Where were the children? She led us into a room with eight beds, all different, but beside each was an identical unpainted low cabinet with half a dozen cubbyholes where the children kept their things.

"You can sleep here," Frau Strom told Ruth. "It's the only bed available. Your sister will be in the next room. It's just as well. When sisters are together they usually fight."

In the next room a girl about my age was sweeping the floor, her long straight hair half falling over her face. She looked up briefly when we came in, then continued with her work.

I glanced around. All the cabinets were filled, except one that stood beside a crib. I looked at Frau Strom.

"We are overcrowded," she said. "The agency doesn't seem to understand that I can't *make* room. I have asked for more beds, but do they send them? Well, you're not so very tall. You'll fit. Put your things in the shelf, then. Emma, did you sweep under the beds?" she asked the girl.

"Yes," the girl said softly, pushing back her hair.

"Here, then." Frau Strom held out a chocolate bar, and the girl took it quickly. "Unpack your things, Lisa!" Frau Strom said, and I was surprised that she knew my name.

As soon as Frau Strom was gone, Emma began eating greedily, taking large bites of the chocolate.

"When is lunch?" I asked her.

"You missed it."

I began to unpack, and Emma watched me, still eating.

"I'm Lisa Platt," I told her, not at all sure that she cared.

"How do you do," she said with some sarcasm. "I'm Emma. Emma, the housemaid."

"What do you mean?"

"My wages," she said, holding out what was left of the chocolate bar. "Would you like some?"

"No thanks."

"Take a little piece, Lisa."

I accepted, and immediately longed for more, but it was gone. "Where are the others?" I asked.

"Out playing in the woods, I guess," Emma said. She fixed her keen blue eyes on me intently. "There's nothing to do here, you know."

"But what about Frau Strom?"

"What about her? She doesn't do anything either, except curl her hair and go out shopping. It's like a jail, you see. The worst thing about a jail," she said, pushing back her long hair, "is that there's nothing to do. We're all just waiting."

"For what?"

"Oh, different things. Some are waiting to leave Switzerland. I'm waiting to be adopted. Big chance—people only want babies. What are you waiting for?"

"To be with my father in America," I said.

"Ah well, that is something worthwhile, at least. You won't mind it here," she said, smiling slightly. "The other kids aren't bad. Say, do you play the piano?"

I shook my head. "I dance, though."

"There's one boy here, Werner, who plays the piano. He won't do it anymore, though. Too many keys are stuck on that old thing in the parlor. We call Werner the professor. There's nothing to do, but he's always busy. He studies things, like bugs and flowers and rocks. I wish I could be that way," she said wistfully. "I'm too restless." She began to pace, as if to prove her words, and by her attitude it seemed that the only thing lacking were bars on the windows.

Ruth came in, looking as confused as I felt, asking, "Where is everybody?"

"Ruth, meet Emma," I said, still unpacking my things.

"What's that crib for?"

"Me." I felt a lump rising in my throat.

"You can take the mattress out," Ruth said at last, "and sleep on the floor."

"No," Emma said briefly. "There are mice."

I couldn't look at either of them. I dreaded the night, and when it came and the little room was noisy with girls all settling down into their beds, I climbed up into the crib. All talk ceased suddenly, and it seemed that everyone avoided looking at me. "Hey!" I cried out, unable to bear their silence. "Look at me!" I clung to the bars and scratched violently and made faces like a monkey. Now there was laughter all around me, and they cried, "Oh, Lisa, do it again! That's the funniest thing I ever saw!"

"Quiet now!" came Frau Strom's voice from the corridor. The lights went out, and I curled up into a sleeping position, the top panel of the crib pressing against my head.

I awakened ravenous. Supper the night before had consisted only of oatmeal and crackers and half an apple for each of us.

"When do we eat?" I asked Emma, climbing out of my bed.

"Never," she replied. "Never enough."

"What do you mean?" I demanded.

"We get oatmeal and beans, oatmeal and crackers,

oatmeal and apples," Emma said, her jaw firm with anger. "Oatmeal is cheap, you see."

"I do *not* see!" I cried, feeling faint from hunger.

"You will," Emma replied.

As Emma had said, oatmeal appeared unfailingly at each meal that day and the next and the next. There was only one helping for each of us.

"Nobody complains," I said to Ruth incredulously.

"Maybe they're used to it," she answered. "But I'm not!" Her face had that look of angry determination I knew so well. "Come on," she said, yanking my arm.

She half pulled me through the dim corridor, and when we stood in front of Frau Strom's door, she knocked loudly. There was no answer, and she knocked again, harder, and we heard a shout, "Come in!"

The radio was blaring, and Frau Strom turned to look at us. "Well, what is it?" she shouted over the noise.

"My sister and I are hungry," Ruth said distinctly. "We would like something to eat."

Frau Strom stared at us, and her face turned redder still, as if she could not believe her ears. Deliberately she walked to the radio and turned it off, then faced Ruth. "What did you say?"

"We're hungry," Ruth repeated. "May we have something to eat?"

"I saw it from the first," said Frau Strom, her eyes blazing. "It shows in your face. You are a typical troublemaker. Have you not eaten three meals every day since you arrived? Do you hear any of the other children complaining? At least they are not rude. At least they have some gratitude. Did you expect the Ritz Hotel? This is a charity camp. *Charity!*" She almost screamed the word, and my hands were trembling.

"It's no good to give charity to some people," she went on, breathing heavily. "They're never satisfied. Well, I will tell you something, young lady. You will appreciate what you have here, and if you should dare to come to this room again asking for special favors," her voice shook with anger, and she stepped close to Ruth, "if you should dare, you will be punished. In other countries children are starving and you—you—*get out*!"

We fled, the door slamming after us, Ruth sobbing while I tried in vain to comfort her. Ruth flung herself down on her bed, and I sat down beside her. At last Ruth looked up, her face red and tearstained, and she said between clenched teeth, "She steals the money the agency sends for our food. She uses it to buy clothes."

"Oh, Ruth," I began, and then we heard Emma's calm voice from the doorway.

"It's true, of course," Emma said. "She goes to town two or three times a week and comes back with boxes and boxes of clothes. She's going again this afternoon. She had Pop get the car out for her. It's our luck when she goes."

"What do you mean?" Ruth asked, wiping her eyes.

"Pop will give us something to eat when she's

gone. He can never refuse us. He's a nice old man, but a little bit . . ." She tapped her finger on her forehead. "You know, strange."

As soon as Frau Strom's car was out of sight, all of us as if on signal walked down to the kitchen, with Emma and Werner in the lead. For the first time the house rang with the noise of twenty-three boys and girls all talking at once, and there was a great deal of pushing and laughing as we crowded into the kitchen.

Pop turned from the sink, where he was washing a large pot. "Yes, my children, come in, little ones."

There was laughter, for Werner, at sixteen, was nearly as tall as the old man. "Do you have something for us, Pop?" Werner asked gravely.

"Well, chicken I do not have." The old man smiled, his head bobbing. "Nor do I have eggs nor chopped livers. If you had seen the luncheon spread at the Hotel Hofstaader, the buffet filled, and on an ordinary day, without even any dignitaries . . ."

"Do you have some bread, Pop?" Werner asked gently.

Pop opened the pantry and took out a long loaf. "That I have," he said, "and how about some apple-sauce on top?"

He cut a thick slice for each of us and spread it generously with applesauce. "It should have a touch of cinnamon," he said, shaking his head sadly, "but there is none. The agency doesn't pay for frills, Frau Strom always says. A woman quite in a class by herself."

We all laughed, cheered by the food, and Werner said, "Tell us more about the hotel, Pop."

I couldn't understand Werner's interest or the eagerness of the other children as they crowded close around the stool where Pop sat and began dreamily to share his memories.

I noticed then finally that Werner turned and gave a slight nod to two of the other boys. I saw them take off their jackets and move slowly away

JOURNEY TO AMERICA

from the group, circling toward the pantry. They slipped noiselessly into the small storeroom. When they came out, they moved toward the door, holding their jackets, now curiously lumpy, under their arms.

Now the group began to separate, and Werner said, "We'll go outside now, Pop. Thanks for telling us. It sounds very exciting."

"Ah, yes," Pop sighed, nodding and mopping his face. "That was a time, a time to remember."

Once outside, the boys began to run, and the girls, laughing wildly, followed. I was caught up in the excitement and ran with them, not knowing where we were going or why, thinking only how wonderful it was to be running in the sunshine through the woods, feeling the wind in my hair.

WAYS THROUGH THE WOODS

WHEN WE REACHED A SMALL CLEARING, everyone stopped before a circle of large, flat stones.

"What's happening?" I asked Emma, still panting.

"A cookout," Emma replied, smiling. "Come on, let's help gather some twigs."

"What is there to cook?"

"Potatoes."

"We stole them," Werner said, coming up with a large log. "What do you think of that?" he demanded with a nod at Ruth.

Ruth's cheeks reddened, then she quickly looked away.

Soon a fire blazed in the circle of rocks, and we all sat around it until the potatoes were done. They were scorched and burning hot on the outside, half raw on the inside, but we feasted on them hungrily and called them delicious.

I looked around at the faces that had become familiar in just a few days. There were the twins, Nick and Anton, who spoke only Italian but made themselves understood nevertheless. There were Lotte and her brother David, both pale and silent; they had fled from Vienna. We knew nothing more. There was Carla from Holland, always gay, her blond braids swinging. Her parents had sent her to Zurich alone, intending to follow later.

Ruth and I were the lucky ones, with our mother close by. I wondered what my mother and the parents of the others would think if they saw us sitting there eating stolen potatoes. And yet, they must have been intended for us. How could people steal from themselves?

For the first time in many days I felt peaceful and

happy. I began to wander away from the group, thinking of Papa and how he would love the forest. I wanted to memorize it all, to tell him later and let him share it. Just beyond the campfire circle was a field of tiny yellow and pink wildflowers. The wild grass reached up to my knees, and I bent down to let the fragrance surround me. Nearby, in a large fallen log, a colony of insects was working, building, and I stopped to watch. Still farther a clump of willows stood bent together, and between their leaves I could see a stream flowing down the hillside, wearing the large stones into smooth, glistening mounds.

"You like it?"

I was startled, then I smiled at Werner, who stood beneath a tree, closely examining the bark.

"It's beautiful," I sighed. "I didn't know there were so many beautiful places in the world. When we were leaving Germany, I looked out of the train window and I thought it was the end."

"I know." He nodded. "I felt the same. But that's

wrong. There is always something more. Look at this." He motioned for me to come near. "See that perfect circle of holes? A woodpecker sits here every morning and makes these designs. This tree," he said gravely, "is sixty-eight years old."

"How do you know?"

"By counting the rings here where the branch was cut. It was cut with an ax," he said. "You can tell by the marks. See this dark mark and the hollow place?"

I nodded.

"The tree was struck by lightning some years ago, about ten, I think. New shoots are growing all around the scar."

"How do you know these things?" I asked him, feeling awed and privileged to be his pupil.

"I read," he said, "and I think about things. The secret is to concentrate, to forget about yourself."

"Are there books here?" I had not read for weeks, and I longed, now, for something new to fill my mind, as Werner's explanations had done.

"In the parlor," he said, "on the shelf behind the piano there are some books."

"Storybooks?" I asked eagerly.

"No. There are some on wildlife, a few about minerals, and some almanacs. Don't look so sad! Maybe there is a storybook or two. But it doesn't matter. You can read about the wildlife or find facts in the almanac and make up the stories for yourself."

No boy had ever spoken to me this way. Actually, my cousins were the only boys I really knew well, and they were always joking and playing pranks. Werner was much older than I, and yet I felt that he understood me, that he already knew whatever I would say.

"You're from Berlin too, aren't you?" I asked.

"Yes," he said, stepping out into the clearing abruptly. "It's going to rain," he said. "I can feel it. Come on, we'd better get back."

Later, when we were indoors and the rain gushed down against the windows and thunder cracked in the distance, I asked Emma about Werner.

"Do you like him?" she asked with a slow smile.

I shrugged. "He's very smart."

"Yes, he is." Emma nodded. "He knows so many things; mostly he knows about people. I was crying once, and he saw me and we talked. He knew why I was crying, I think, even before I told him. That's when he told me about himself. He's from Berlin, you know. One day he was at a friend's house, and when he went home his parents were gone. He found out later that his father had been shot. He doesn't even know where his mother is. His parents had both spoken out against the Nazis at a meeting. Friends sent him here to Switzerland. I guess he's worse off than any of us, not knowing."

I went down to the parlor and groped along the shelf behind the piano. The parlor was always dark, for there were no bulbs in the light sockets. I took the first book that my hand grasped and sat with it on the stairway, where a dim light shone and the noise from upstairs was muted. It was a very old book about birds. The pages were badly warped, some of them stuck together with mildew, but I read with complete absorption all afternoon and into the night, not realizing until later that there was to be no supper at all.

Perhaps Pop had forgotten, hypnotized by his memories. Perhaps Frau Strom, returning late from the city, happened to investigate the pantry and discovered the half-empty potato bin. Nothing was said, and although my stomach growled, I went to bed contented, calculating how wise I would be if I read a book every single day of my life.

I read almost constantly for the next few days, while outside the rain continued in torrents, and Frau Strom kept to her room, unwilling, as she put it, to catch her death by going to town in the rain. To us it meant simply that there would be no stolen treats, either from the pantry or from Pop.

But one day Frau Strom approached me as I sat on the stair reading a book about Catholic saints. She interrupted just as in my story the torches were being lit around the pyre where St. Joan was tied to the stake.

"Do you have a sweet tooth, Lisa?"

I looked up, startled, and saw that she held out a bar of chocolate.

I nodded, still dazed from the story.

"There is dusting to be done," she said, "and the hall is thick with mud. You would think that people would wipe their feet, wouldn't you?"

My eyes were fastened on the chocolate, a thick, large bar. Suddenly I hated her tight little curls and ruddy face, and the temptation she put in front of me. Oh, I wanted to be a martyr like St. Joan and the others so clearly pictured in the storybook. I wanted desperately to resist the bribe, to cry out that I would not work for the food that certainly we were entitled to receive. But I dearly love sweets, and my mouth watered until I felt faint from the desire.

I stood up and said, "I'll do it."

"You will have your reward when you are finished,"

said Frau Strom, putting the chocolate back in her pocket.

I had never scrubbed before. What happens to the handle while you're wringing out the mop? I had watched Clara do it dozens of times, and I had never seen *her* get sopping wet or getting her feet tangled in the long wooden handle.

I had to laugh at my own awkwardness, but by the time I had finished mopping the long hallway twice over, I was so tired and miserable that I sat down on the stair, feeling truly like a martyr. I dreaded the thought that anyone would walk on that floor. I remembered how Clara used to say, "Now, don't you stamp mud all over my clean kitchen!" But she always said it with a twinkle in her eyes, and she was never really cross. Why hadn't I ever told Clara how much I loved her while there was still time? The last time I said good-bye, I knew I would probably never see Clara again. Now I realized what that meant.

When Frau Strom came to inspect the hallway,

she only nodded and handed me the chocolate, saying, "This is only for you. Don't give any to your sister."

I wouldn't look at her. I wouldn't let her see that I had been crying. She would have thought I was crying about the work—if she had noticed at all—but it was for Clara, only for Clara. I went up and found Ruth and divided the chocolate bar in half.

"Keep it," she said, twisting her hair. "You shouldn't have to work for me. I'm the oldest."

I held it out to her again and again, but Ruth wouldn't budge. At last I ate every bit of the chocolate myself, but it tasted dull and almost sickening. The next time Frau Strom came to me with that forced little smile on her face, offering me candy if I would wash the floor, I shook my head. "I don't like chocolate anymore," I told her.

She went off with a snort. "Stubborn little mule!"

As the days dragged on I realized how right Emma had been, for we were like prisoners with nothing to do, nothing to plan or look forward to. We tried to make up games, and I read a great deal, but all I really thought about was leaving, going back to Mother. Yet, if we went to Zurich for a visit, how could we ever make ourselves return to the camp?

When the rains were finally over, Ruth decided we should go to see Mother.

"Can we?" I cried. "Will Frau Strom let us?"

"She won't care," Ruth replied. "The woman at the agency said we could visit."

"But how do we get there?"

"We'll walk," Ruth said. "Emma told me the way. She's walked to Zurich several times. We just go straight through the woods—there's a dirt road behind the campfire place. Past the woods there are some houses, then a paved road leads right into the city. It's really a shortcut," she explained. "It should take us only an hour or so."

"I still think we should tell Frau Strom," I insisted.

"Tell her if you like," Ruth said. "She won't care."

Ruth was right.

"Go ahead," Frau Strom said with a wave of her hand. "You'd better be back by dark, because nobody is going to come out looking for you."

I couldn't stand to wait another moment. "Let's go now," I begged Ruth.

"We'll miss lunch," Ruth reminded me.

"I don't care. It's only porridge anyway. I can't stand the sight of it anymore."

"All right," Ruth agreed. But on the way she warned me again and again, "Don't you say a word to Mother about being hungry, do you understand? Don't you say a word about the oatmeal or the potatoes."

"I won't," I muttered, wanting only to enjoy the walk and the thought of seeing Mother, but still Ruth lectured.

"Mother can't afford to keep us with her, you know that. If she thinks we're not getting enough to eat, she'll feel that she ought to keep us in Zurich, and then she'll worry, and then . . ."

⋆⋆★ 121 ★⋆⋆

"Oh, stop it," I snapped. "I won't say anything."

We made our way through the woods, careful to keep to the narrow dirt path. I was afraid of getting lost out in the forest, and I think Ruth was too, for she kept chattering incessantly. The sudden, cackling call of a large bird made us jump, and then we laughed at our foolishness. Midway down the mountain we came upon a small log cabin, leaning downhill as if with the next big windstorm it would collapse completely. On the roof was a short chimney of stones, and the door had a hole where the latch had once been.

Ruth and I gazed at each other, our feet still firmly on the path. "Just an old cabin," she said, sounding very, very uninterested. "Some old woodsman probably used it."

"Yes," I said. "We'd better go on. We still have a long walk ahead of us."

But still I looked at that dark cabin, wishing so very much for the courage to go inside, horrified at the things my imagination told me lay behind that door, ashamed of the dryness in my throat and of my terror.

"I can't go in," I whispered to Ruth.

"Who said you should? Come on. Don't be silly."

Still I brooded, until we came upon the small cluster of houses that showed we were at the city's edge. Then we ran the rest of the way down the hill, faster and faster, until at last the streets were familiar, the distant mountains, the lake, the shops exactly the same as before. I felt, suddenly, that we had been away for months. It had been less than three weeks.

"Remember," Ruth told me sternly when we approached the rooming house, "not a word."

Annie's shouts and hugs and tears and Mother's kisses made it seem that we had truly been gone a long time.

"Oh, tell me about the camp," Annie cried, climbing onto my lap. "Are there games? Are there stories? Do you get to swim?"

"No," I said. "No swimming."

Ruth spoke about the other girls and where they

were from, and I told about the forest and the flowers and streams, but then there was nothing more to tell.

"You're probably tired from the long walk," Mother said. She looked at us intently, and all through the afternoon it seemed that she was about to ask a question, but then she would only sigh and shake her head and press my hand or Ruth's. Finally she went to the little kitchen and asked cheerfully, "Are you hungry?"

"No," Ruth said quickly in a loud voice.

"Did you have lunch?"

"Oh yes," I said.

"I went to the market this morning and bought a nice German sausage," Mother said. "I was going to fix some anyway, with eggs. Won't you try a little?"

The smell of that sausage frying was overpowering. We sat down at the table.

"Come on, Ruth," Mother coaxed, "eat."

"Well, just a little," Ruth said softly, flushing.

"Just a little for me, too," I added. I was, I thought

in disgust, becoming a glutton, thinking of nothing but food.

When we had finished, Mother took me aside, and I was afraid for a moment that she would ask a question that I would not be able to answer without telling a direct lie. But she only handed me an envelope, saying, "This letter from Rosemarie came for you a few days ago."

I looked for a long moment at Rosemarie's handwriting, the letters so round and neat. Then I went to sit by the window and opened it.

My dearest Lisa,

I was so happy to get your letter. How pretty Zurich must be from your description. I can really picture it all, the lake, the hills, the houses. Wouldn't it be wonderful if we were there together? Can you send me some postcards?

I glanced up and saw that Mother and Ruth busied themselves in the tiny kitchen, leaving me alone with my precious letter. How would I explain to Rosemarie that I had no money to buy picture postcards?

The summer seems very long without you. Mother says I keep to myself too much, and I have tried going places with some of the other girls, but it just isn't the same. So I read a lot, and I have been painting again.

I hear that Hanna and her parents have left the city. I don't know where they went. My parents speak of taking a trip someday, maybe to Palestine. Wouldn't it be wonderful to see Jerusalem? But for now Father is so busy with his patients that he can't even think of it.

I knew how it was for Rosemarie, that her parents would sit up late into the night puzzling over what to do, whether to leave, whether to stay, as my parents had sat up talking and wondering.

For myself I'd be happy never to see or hear our "off-key chimpanzees" again.

It was our private name for those brown-shirted students who went through the streets singing their hateful songs. They seemed to us like apes, and Rosemarie and I used to scorn them in private, "They swing their arms like chimpanzees, and they sing off-key!"

I was in the park roller-skating one day last week, and a group of the apes came along, shouting and calling insults to an old man. You must know what names they called him. They told him to get down on his hands and knees and pick up the papers there in the park—that old, old man. And when he just stood there, shaking and confused, they started reaching into the trash can and they threw the garbage at him, but still the old man couldn't move. They closed in on him, and I knew they were going to beat him. Lisa, what could I do? I felt so sick inside. How could I help that man?

I saw what they were doing to him, but the old man didn't even cry out. What good would it have done? A group of little kids came running up, and they stood there watching, as if it were an entertainment. I couldn't stand it, and I ran home. I must have been pretty hysterical. For the first time in my life I was sick to my stomach. I shouted at my mother to call the police. Then I realized that there are no policemen that we can call.

I read over this letter and I realize how dismal I must sound, but you know I'm never sad for long. I'm sure everything will be fine. Fifi says to tell you, "Go out and play!"

I smiled to myself, remembering Fifi, her parrot, who always, at any time of the day or night, shouted in that peculiar voice, "Go out and play!" and for some inexplicable reason added, "Dirty dishes! Dirty dishes!"

I showed Mother the letter, and she read it, her lips pressed tightly together. "Rosemarie should be careful of what she writes," Mother said softly. "If only they would decide to . . ." But she left the thought unfinished and asked me instead, "When do you have to be back?"

"Before dark," I told her, remembering Frau Strom's warning.

"Then we have time," Mother said, "to take that ride up the Uetliberg. Annie's been waiting so eagerly."

I had never been on a funicular. We stood at the little station house and looked up, straight up, to where the cable climbed the mountainside to the top and out of sight. It seemed unbelievable that the little car would actually be pulled up that mountain clear to the top.

People piled in, the four of us sitting close together, and when the climb began we looked down, clutching at each other, laughing and gasping, for never in this world was there a mountain so steep or a car so rickety making its way upward like a determined alpine goat. The houses and people below shrank smaller and smaller, and I kept my eyes fastened on them, determined not to miss the thrill, though my stomach felt as if I were riding an elevator clear up to the sky.

The car creaked to a stop, and we all rushed out into the cold air, giggling with excitement. How clear it was! All of Zurich lay at our feet, the boats on the lake were tiny white dots, the houses like mere wooden blocks of different colors, and the people— they were not to be seen at all. "We're the only people in the world!" I exclaimed, laughing. "It's wonderful."

"I can see clear to America!" Annie shouted. "Papa!" she called, as if she were inside a cave. "Hello-oo."

The ride down seemed shorter, but no less exciting, and when we arrived I felt that we had been up in a balloon and back again.

Too soon it was time to go back, and Mother and Annie walked with us to the houses where the real climb began. Then Annie hugged us and called, "Come back. Come back soon." Mother kissed us solemnly, and I wondered that she did not say, as usually she did, "Be good. Remember all you've been taught."

Three days later I knew why. Frau Strom came into the dormitory and said in a rigid voice, "Pack your things, Lisa. Your mother is here."

"Why?" I exclaimed. "What's the matter?"

"Pack your things. You're leaving."

ERICA

A TAXI WAITED OUTSIDE. IN A MOMENT OUR bags were put into the trunk, the car turned around, and we barely had time to wave to the boys and girls who stood curiously at the windows.

"What is it!" I exclaimed, feeling caught up in confusion. Mother had barely spoken to Frau Strom, but rushed us into the taxi and away. "Are we leaving Switzerland? Did Papa send for us?"

"No, darling. I couldn't leave you at that place."

"What do you mean?" Ruth stammered. "We didn't—we didn't say anything."

"You didn't have to," Mother replied. "A mother

knows. Don't you think I could see that you weren't getting enough to eat? No routine, no care at all—like little lost souls, all those children looking out of the windows!" She took up her handkerchief and wiped her eyes, hard, as if some speck of dust irritated them.

I felt numb from the abruptness of our departure. "Where's Annie?" I asked, wanting her, somehow, to make it seem real.

"When I went to the agency and told them that I was taking you away from the camp," Mother said, "they gave me the names of several families who have offered to take children to live with them for a while. I went to see one of the families this morning. They want Annie to stay with them."

"Tell me about them," I said, trying to conceal my disappointment.

"I had to send her, Lisa," Mother said seriously. "Don't think I wanted to let her go. But I haven't been feeling very strong lately, and Annie needs playmates too." She sighed.

"Do they have children?" I could imagine Annie playing and laughing, and I wanted her with me.

"There are children Annie's age next door to the Zeilers," Mother told me. "They have a baby boy. Actually, Frau Zeiler wanted an older child; but when she saw Annie and talked to her, she couldn't bear to let her go. And Annie was happy to stay."

"What about us?" Ruth asked, biting her lip.

"I have found homes for you," Mother said. "It won't be for long, I hope. Papa has saved almost enough money to buy our tickets. You'll be staying with families right here in Zurich. You'll be able to visit me as much as you like."

All that afternoon and late into the evening we sat in the little room talking, and this time Ruth and I told everything. Mother listened, shaking her head, now and then reaching for her handkerchief, murmuring, "Oh, why didn't you tell me? What if I hadn't suspected?"

Now I began to think of Emma and Werner and

all the others who had no place to go, nobody who would come for them.

"I keep thinking about the others," I said hesitantly, "that we should do something."

"What can I possibly do?" Mother asked wearily. "I can report this to the agency, and there will be an investigation, I suppose, but such things take time. And probably at the end they'll say, 'Well, it's not a perfect place for children, but it's the best we can do right now.'" Mother sighed deeply. "There are too many needs, too few people who know and want to help. Well, I'll make the report, girls. We'll see if something comes of it."

But we all knew that we were completely helpless to bring any real change.

To sleep that night in the spacious double bed beside Ruth was like a special gift. I had never been so happy before simply to go to bed and stretch out, and to turn without bumping my head or my elbows. I said to Ruth, "How wonderful to sleep in a real bed!" Mother heard, and for some reason this, more than anything we had told her, made her break down and weep.

"I'm so sorry, so sorry," she said again and again. "I shouldn't have sent you. I didn't know. You don't deserve this, really, such good children."

I made my voice light. "Oh, so what. It didn't hurt me. Actually, it was funny. Imagine me in a crib, at my age!" I made my monkey faces, and Mother began to smile faintly, and then she kissed us good night.

We did not even unpack our clothes the next morning, for we were to go to the agency that afternoon, to meet the families that would be taking care of us. After breakfast Mother asked us to go to the grocery store for her.

"I've made out the shopping list," she said, "but I think I'd rather stay here and rest a little. I feel so tired," she added apologetically.

"It's all right," Ruth and I said. "We like to shop."

We got our coats and the money, but just as we

reached the door Mother called out in a strange, trembling voice, "Oh, don't go, girls! I need you. I feel so—so . . ."

We rushed toward her, for Mother was moving unsteadily toward the bed, and then her body seemed to crumple, and she lay on the floor, motionless.

Ruth crouched beside her calling, "Mother! Mother! Mother!" and I raced down the stairs, shouting for Frau Feldin. My heart made loud thumps in my ears, and I heard my own voice as a strange, dull sound as I pounded on Frau Feldin's door. "A doctor! Get a doctor! My mother has fainted."

I had never seen anybody faint, but I knew, and somehow I knew what to do. Something inside moved me without my willing it or thinking of it. I stood beside Frau Feldin while she screeched her message into the telephone. Then I went upstairs. Somehow Mother had gotten onto the bed, conscious now, her hand reaching out slowly toward Ruth, who knelt beside the bed looking completely dazed.

"I'll be all right, Ruth," I heard Mother whisper.

I threw open the window to let in some fresh air. I took off Mother's shoes and she sighed faintly. Then I began, mechanically, to put the kettle on for some tea, and I gave Mother a cold cloth for her head.

"Thank you, Lisa," she whispered, reaching again toward Ruth, who still had not moved from the spot.

I was feeding Mother spoonfuls of hot tea when we heard voices coming from the stairs, Frau Feldin's high-pitched, distracted chatter, and the strong, calm voice of the doctor.

When he stepped into the room, I suddenly felt that I had always known him, and that he knew us, knew exactly what we felt and needed. He filled the room completely, moving about as if all this were most natural and familiar. He was not a tall man, but broad-shouldered and solidly built. His face was deeply creased, and his eyes were keen with life, his hair and eyebrows thick and shaggy. I wanted to go to him, but I waited.

He felt Mother's pulse, then took her temperature and asked to wash his hands. I ran to get a clean towel, and he smiled and put his arm briefly around my shoulder.

"I'm Dr. Gross," he said.

"I'm Lisa Platt," I told him, "and this is my sister Ruth." I waved toward Ruth, and he went to her, touching her face gently. "Go and sit down on the sofa now, Ruth," he said softly. "I must have room to tend to your mother. Go, child. I'll take care of your mother. You needn't be afraid."

Ruth moved to the sofa, and we sat there together, watching Dr. Gross.

"When did you eat last?" he asked Mother.

"Breakfast," Mother murmured. "I had a cup of tea."

"No more," he stated, shaking his head. "I'm afraid you have a touch of pneumonia, Frau Platt. It probably began with an ordinary cold and you must have been under considerable strain."

"Yes," Mother whispered. "We are from Germany—refugees."

"I understand," he said. "Don't try to talk now. I'm going to send for an ambulance to take you to the hospital," he said in his deep, steady voice. "It's nothing to be alarmed about, just a convenience. I know you're feeling very weak, Frau Platt, and it probably hurts a bit when you try to breathe deeply, doesn't it?"

Mother only nodded, and her eyes filled with tears.

"The children," she whispered. "They were supposed to go to stay with some people this afternoon. The addresses are in my purse. The Resettlement Agency . . ."

"I'll call the agency and inform them," said the doctor. "We'll arrange to have your girls taken care of. Now you rest for a moment while I talk to Lisa."

"Where is your father?" he asked me softly.

"In America," I replied. "And my little sister, Annie, is staying with another family."

"Your mother will be in the hospital for several weeks," Dr. Gross said, frowning. "But she'll be all right."

"Will we be able to visit?" I asked.

"Not for a while. It's contagious. It's a wonder you and your sister haven't caught it."

I explained that we had just returned from camp, pointing to our suitcases still unpacked.

"Well, you're certainly having your share of experiences," he said, and I was thankful that he did not sympathize. It would have made me cry.

He turned to Ruth. "Are you better now? Your mother is in no danger. I'm going to see to it that she receives the best possible care, that she gets lots of rest and good food. You'll be able to telephone her every day."

"I'm all right now," Ruth said, standing very straight. "Thank you."

Mother asked me to find the note in her purse. On it were written two names, "family Kunst and family Werfel." My name was written beside the latter.

"You will like it," Mother whispered to me. "I met Herr Werfel. He has a daughter too."

The next few hours passed in a haze, with the ambulance sending its terrible wail along the streets, doctors in white coats rushing in with a stretcher, Mother reaching out to touch our faces as they took her away. I felt that somehow I had lived all this before, and my body responded automatically, without feeling.

"How can you be so calm?" Ruth asked me again and again, as we walked to the agency office, where we were to meet the people who were taking us to their homes. Mother had forgotten to leave money for bus fare, and we hadn't thought to ask. "How can you be so calm? My whole body is shaking."

"I don't know," I replied.

"I wish we could be together," she said, biting her lip.

"I'll call you tonight," I promised.

"Mother said they have a boy my age," Ruth told me. "I don't want to go."

I laughed slightly. "He won't bother you. Don't you like boys?"

"Don't tease now, Lisa," she said gravely. "You

know what I mean. Oh, this suitcase is heavy. I feel like a gypsy."

I still felt nothing at all. I might have been watching from a distance. It was the same feeling I had the night Papa left, that the real me was only looking on. I put one foot in front of the other until we reached the agency office, and suddenly I found myself in the arms of the tall, graying man who was Herr Werfel.

"My child!" he exclaimed. "Come, let me take that suitcase. They didn't tell us you had to walk all this way. Come, come to the car, my dear. We'll take you home."

Ruth, too, was leaving, walking beside a tall, thin boy, speaking with him shyly. She turned back to wave good-bye and I knew that she was satisfied to go.

In the car something inside me gave way. I began to tremble violently, and tears slid down my cheeks, although I hardly realized I was crying.

Frau Werfel put her arms around me, and I lay against her while she murmured, "There, there. Let it all go, my child. Don't try to hold back. There is a time for tears now, now all will be well."

I looked up at last and saw their daughter, Erica, looking at me with such consternation that I had to smile. "I'm fine," I said. "Really, I'm sorry."

"When we get home," Erica said with a smile that made her whole face glow, "I'll show you the rabbits. We have eight altogether, six babies. We keep them in the barn. Would you like to have one of the bunnies to keep?"

I didn't know what to say, and she continued, "We can sleep together in my room—if you want to, that is."

"I want to," I said. She was so sweet, not pretty like Rosemarie, but her face was so frank and filled with feeling that I knew we would be friends, really friends, although she was nearly two years younger than I.

"Let Lisa rest awhile," Frau Werfel told Erica when we reached the large old farmhouse. "Lie down here on the sofa, dear. Erica, don't tire Lisa with too

much talk. We'll have many days together, I hope."
She bent down and kissed me, as if I were her own. I
looked from one to the other, at Frau Werfel's plump,
motherly face, at Herr Werfel, tall as a reed, but
gentle in his movements, and I could see that they
really wanted me.

The sofa was old and comfortable, like the house
itself. I lay down against the soft cushions, and Erica
sat beside me, fingering her long dark braids and
smiling but not speaking.

"I have never been on a farm," I told her. "What
do you grow?"

"It's not really much of a farm," Erica said. "We
have a few chickens and pigs, and a vegetable garden."

"Do you have a horse?"

"Oh yes. There's the barn, you see, and it wouldn't
do to leave it empty, so we got the horse."

I laughed slightly. She was so serious, so eager to
please, it seemed.

"My cousins live just up the hill," she said. "They

have a large apple orchard. I'll take you there one day, and you can drink all the apple cider you want. And you can ride the horse if you like horses, which I guess you do, because you asked about it. We have a hayloft. Have you ever been in a hayloft? Oh, there are a few little mice under the hay, but they won't bother you. Sometimes you can hear them squeak, and sometimes they pop out, but then they run away and hide again very quickly."

She gazed at me for a long moment. "Do you want to sleep? Am I talking too much?"

"No, not at all."

"I don't suppose you play with dolls," she said. "I don't either, never did much. I've always had little animals, instead, like the bunnies. Do you like to play ball?"

I nodded.

"I do too. It's something you can do alone. There aren't many children in the neighborhood. That's why I'm so glad you came to stay with us. It must have been exciting to live in Berlin. I have always lived right here."

Frau Werfel came in with mugs of hot chocolate. "Erica!" she reprimanded. "You're talking too much." But her eyes were gay, and she said to me, "I can't really blame her. We're all so excited about having you with us."

Frau Werfel thought of everything. After dinner she telephoned the hospital, and I was allowed to talk to Mother, but only for a few minutes.

"Do you like the Werfels?" she asked me in a soft, weak voice.

"Yes, yes," I assured her, "very much."

She sighed. "I have a nice room," she said. "The nurses bring me food every two hours." She paused, as if speaking were an effort. "The doctor says I'm undernourished. But I'll be well soon," she added hastily. "Be a good girl, Lisa, and remember— remember all you have been taught."

I went into the kitchen, where Frau Werfel was

setting out bread dough to rise overnight. Her move-ments as she kneaded the dough and the smell of yeast reminded me of home and of all the times I had sat at the kitchen table watching Clara.

From the next room I could hear Erica and her father talking softly, laughing now and then. There was music from the radio, a pretty tune I had never heard before, but somehow everything seemed familiar, too familiar. I was not really a part of it. How could I be? I could belong to only one fam-ily, and mine was scattered in different directions. I knew that I was wanted here, and welcome, but my mind and heart were divided into too many places, and I could not feel whole.

Frau Werfel turned to smile at me. "Would you like to write to your father, Lisa? I've put out some statio-nery and stamps. You can sit here at the kitchen table."

I thanked her, marveling that she seemed to know just how I felt. I had wanted to write to Papa for weeks, but had not been able to for lack of paper and a stamp.

It grew dark outside while I wrote, but I was too engrossed to notice anything around me. I gave no thought whatever to the organization of my letter. I simply wrote and wrote, leaping from one thing to the other, from one place to another, but always picturing Papa here beside me.

When at last I was finished, Herr Werfel called to me. "Come and sit with us awhile, Lisa," he said. "Tell us about your family. Tell us about your father."

I began slowly, almost reluctantly. How could I possibly describe Papa? I told them some of the funny little stories Papa had told me, never make-believe stories, but real incidents that happened to him. He had told me many things about his childhood, and I could picture him and his four brothers turning the house inside out with their pranks. I told of the time when Papa, as a young boy, had eaten nearly a whole bushel of cherries, just to prove to his brothers that he could do it. I told how, at the age of fourteen, he was apprenticed to a tailor in another town, and how he ran back home one night, overcome with loneliness. I told about the time Papa had invented a new cleaning fluid, and how the bottle had exploded in the garage. And I told how, before our trip to Brazil, Papa had to go to Czechoslovakia to pick up Ruth from boarding school.

"He needed money to pay for her school and to get to Italy, but he wasn't allowed to take any money out. He had to hide it in some way."

Herr Werfel nodded, and Erica asked, "What did he do?"

"He bought some grapes," I answered. "He put them in a double bag, with money between the two bags. When the inspector came onto the train, Papa was sitting there eating grapes. He offered some to the inspector, too."

"What if he had been caught?" Erica gasped.

"He would have gone to jail, I guess," I said. "But he's a good actor, my father. Oh, he can make anybody laugh!"

I felt closer to Papa than ever, and when it was time to go to bed, I was contented and whole.

Frau Werfel had unpacked my clothes and laid my pajamas out on the bed beside Erica's. My dresses were hung neatly in Erica's closet, and now I saw how shabby they had become. I got into bed quickly, self-conscious about the patches on my pajamas.

Frau Werfel did not seem to notice. She kissed us both, then tucked the blankets around me, saying, "Good night, Lisa dear. We're so lucky to have you with us."

I watched as Erica knelt beside her bed to say her prayers, and I looked up at the picture of Jesus, the shepherd, that hung on the wall. When she had finished, Erica turned to me with her glowing smile and said, "Good night."

What was it, I wondered, that made these people so good?

In the darkness I said my own prayer, ending as always, "and please let us all be together again soon."

QUESTIONS AND QUOTAS

IT HAD BEEN A WONDERFUL WEEK, EACH day filled with new, exciting things to do. I rode the horse every morning, a sweet, gentle old mare that had probably never received a cross word in her life. Her name was Stella, for she had a white patch, almost the shape of a star on her forehead. Sweet Stella, I called her, as she rubbed her nose against my hands and clothing, searching for the carrots and sugar lumps we always brought.

That week opened a new world to me. Who in Berlin had ever picked peas fresh from the garden, or gathered eggs in a henhouse? How could I ever have dreamed that a hayloft could be such a marvelous place for play, or for lying down and looking out of the loft window, or for jumping down onto the slippery, fresh-smelling stacks below?

I had never seen apples growing on trees. I had certainly never seen a cider press. We trooped up the hill, Erica and I, to her cousin's house, about a mile along the country road, and then we went into the orchards, where the apples hung ripe on the trees and bushel baskets of picked fruit stood in rows. We brought a gallon jug with us, and Frau Werfel always said with a twinkling smile, "Now this time bring the cider *home*." Erica's aunt would fill the jug with cider, and on the way down the hill we were always tempted to take just a little taste, then another and another, passing the jug back and forth, until when we arrived back at Erica's house the jug was empty. "Now go back," Erica's mother would say, giving her a playful swat, "and this time bring the cider *home*, you imps!"

Then the last week before school would begin arrived. There is something about that last week of vacation—it is always the very best time of the whole summer. I remarked about it to Erica. "Haven't you found it so?"

"Only since you are here," she answered, giving me a smile. "I wish . . ." She stopped abruptly.

"What do you wish?" I urged her.

"It's selfish of me," she said wistfully. "But I—I wish you could stay with us for a long, long time."

I didn't want to think beyond that day.

"Do you think your mother will let you stay with us," Erica asked hesitantly, "until you leave Switzerland?"

"I think so," I replied.

"My father will ask her today," Erica said, for that afternoon they were taking me to the hospital to visit Mother. I had spoken to Dr. Gross on the telephone.

"Yes, I think it would be good for your mother to

see you girls," he had said, "but only one at a time, and just for a few minutes. She still needs plenty of rest."

Dr. Gross was in Mother's room when we arrived. I was struck with how fragile Mother looked in the great bed among the white linens and wearing a hospital gown. I rushed to her, but she held me away. "Not too close, darling. I don't want to take any chances. Sit down there on the chair. Let me look at you. Your cheeks are rosy again!" She smiled and her eyes shone.

"Your mother's getting along fine," Dr. Gross said, taking up his bag. "She'll be up and around in ten days or so, but," he turned to Mother, "you'll still have to take it easy, and remember that people can't live on tea and toast—not if they want to stay healthy."

"I'll remember, Doctor," Mother said meekly, half smiling.

"And you'd best try to keep your daughters right where they are. No use shuffling those girls around like library books!"

"And what would I do all day?" Mother asked him boldly.

"You'll visit them," the doctor said promptly, patting me on the shoulder as he turned to go. "Just a few minutes, now, Lisa."

The Werfels had left me at the door to Mother's room, unwilling to tire her with too many visitors. They were to come back for me in ten minutes. My head was filled with things I wanted to say, but in my rush to tell everything I was, for a moment, speechless.

"You like the Werfels, don't you?" Mother asked.

"They are the most wonderful people I've ever known," I replied promptly. "Frau Werfel made me some pajamas to match Erica's. She said it would be fun for us to have something alike, as if we were real sisters. She's so kind!" Frau Werfel never made it seem that she was giving me a gift or supplying something I desperately needed. It was the same when she made us each dresses. "She says it's just as easy to make two," I told Mother. "How can that be?"

Mother laughed, and her face looked pink and healthy again. "Have you been helping around the house?"

"Oh yes," I said quickly. "But it's fun. I mean, we get to feed the chickens, and Frau Werfel taught me how to darn socks. I made the *nicest* little patch in one of Herr Werfel's."

"Marvelous!" Mother exclaimed. "You're turning into a young lady after all. And today? What did you do today?"

I took a deep breath, then said rapidly, "We went to church. I—I went too. Is it all right?"

"Of course it is," Mother said, nodding.

"The Werfels are Catholic," I said.

"I know."

"It was a Catholic mass," I explained insistently.

"You can pray wherever you are," Mother said soberly, "and still be a good Jew. God is everywhere. I have prayed in many churches. But what's the matter, Lisa? Were you uncomfortable?"

"No," I murmured. "It was beautiful." I sighed, not wanting to ask, but needing to talk about the thoughts that had haunted me. "Do you think that's what makes them so good? Going to church, I mean, and being Catholic?" Our eyes met intently, and there was silence for a moment. Then Mother lay back against the pillows, hesitating before she faced me fully and asked, "What do *you* think?"

"I don't know," I said, shaking my head. I did not ask that nagging question, If I were a Catholic, would I be better too? How could I ask it, even of myself? I loved the synagogue, the songs and prayers, the closeness to God. How could I question the faith of my fathers?

There wasn't time to pursue it, for a nurse came bustling into the room. "There's a letter for you, Frau Platt," she said.

"A letter? But it's Sunday."

"Special delivery," the nurse answered briskly, already on her way out. "From America."

Mother ripped open the envelope.

"Is it from Papa?" I asked, rushing to see.

"Of course." Mother quickly scanned the page, then she cried out, "Oh no! He mustn't."

"What? What is it?"

"Papa says—he—he wants to leave America!" she said in a stricken tone. "He mustn't! He says he got a letter from you and one from Frau Feldin, saying that I was very sick and in the hospital. Lisa, what did you write to Papa?" Her voice was shaking.

"I don't remember, exactly. I told him about Erica."

"What did you say about me?" Mother demanded fiercely. "Tell me!"

"Just that you are sick and in the hospital. Just what you told me, and what Dr. Gross said. I told him you would get better soon. I *told* him you were getting special care and medicine to make you better."

"That Frau Feldin, such a scatterbrain. I never should have given her Papa's address. It was only in case of an emergency."

"She probably thought it *was* an emergency!" I exclaimed. "With the ambulance coming and everything. Wouldn't *you* have thought so?"

"Lisa, for heaven's sake, don't argue with me now. I have to stop him. He says he's making arrangements to come to Zurich. Listen," she read from the letter, "'Benjamin says I am a fool even to think of leaving, but I must come to you and take my chances. I can't sleep for worrying about you, Margo, thinking of you alone in a foreign city and sick. No matter what happens, at least we'll be together. I can't stand . . .'"

She put the letter down, her eyes brimming.

The very thought of seeing Papa filled me with such great excitement that I couldn't think of anything else. Why couldn't he come? Why couldn't we all stay in Switzerland and make it our home? Why America?

"Let him come," I begged, half kneeling beside Mother's bed. "Oh, please, don't stop him."

Mother sat upright and snapped, "Don't be foolish, Lisa. You just don't understand. We can't stay in Zurich. There would be no work for Papa here. Switzerland is a tiny country. They can't take immigrants, and it's too close, too close to Germany."

"You mean the Nazis might come *here*?" I cried.

"I don't know." Mother shook her head, then took my hand gently. "I'm sorry, darling. It wasn't your fault—that Frau Feldin, stupid woman! I'll send a cablegram to Papa," she said. "Ring for the nurse."

When the nurse came, she shook her head firmly. "You are not allowed to get out of bed, Frau Platt."

"Nonsense!" Mother scolded, swinging her feet onto the floor. "Hand me my robe, Lisa."

"It is against my orders," the nurse said, standing in Mother's way. "I'd have to check with Dr. Gross. Now you wait here, Frau Platt," she said. "I'll try to find him."

Mother sat back on the bed. "I'll wait five minutes," she said firmly. "That's all."

"Now just relax," the nurse soothed. "Look, you've

another visitor." She whispered something to Herr Werfel and he nodded, then strode over to Mother and took her hand.

"*Grüss Gott,*" he said, smiling. "I hope you're feeling better, Frau Platt. Oh, your Lisa is a jewel. We want to keep her with us, if we may, until you leave Switzerland. But you look troubled, and the nurse said I am to keep you here. What is it? What can I do?"

When he had heard about the letter, Herr Werfel began to pace back and forth, frowning deeply. "You're right, of course," he said to Mother. "If he once leaves America, your husband may have a hard time reentering. In fact, I've just read in the newspapers about the quota system, and how many people are waiting to go to the United States."

"That's exactly it," Mother said quickly. "As long as my husband is there already, the girls and I don't have to come under the quota system. If he were to leave now, the whole thing would have to be started over again, with new forms, new waiting lists. Now all he has to do is send one more certificate. Oh, Herr Werfel," Mother said pleadingly, "we've waited so long. Everything we've waited for would be undone!"

The nurse came to the door to announce, "Dr. Gross has left the hospital, I'm afraid. You just have to . . ."

"Never mind," Herr Werfel told her. "Frau Platt just wants to send a cablegram. I'll take care of it for her."

He pulled the chair over beside Mother's bed and took a small notebook and pencil from his vest pocket. "Now, take your time," he said gently. "I'll write down exactly what you want to say, and I'll ask for an answer immediately, so you won't have to worry. It will take a few hours, but at least you'll be able to sleep tonight in peace."

Together they composed the message. DO NOT LEAVE AMERICA. RECOVERING QUICKLY. ALL IS WELL. LOVE. MARGO.

"You have more than ten words," Herr Werfel said. "You can omit the word 'love,' or pay extra for it."

"I'll pay extra," Mother said, smiling slightly. "It's worth it."

"I agree," Herr Werfel smiled. "I'll ask for a reply immediately."

"Lie down again now, Mother," I coaxed, and by the time Herr Werfel returned she was settled once more under the blankets, but I knew she would not rest easily until she had Papa's reply.

"We'd better leave you now, Frau Platt," Herr Werfel said. "Try to rest. We'll call you tonight. Oh, I nearly forgot, and Erica will be waiting to know. May I tell her that Lisa will stay with us until you leave?"

"Of course," Mother said gratefully. "You are so kind."

Erica and Frau Werfel were waiting in the car, and now we told them what had happened. "We'll call the hospital right after supper," Frau Werfel said. But it was not until after our third call that we knew Papa's answer. "Will stay. Sending last form this month. Love to girls."

"It's long past bedtime," Frau Werfel announced, "and you two have school tomorrow."

But neither Erica nor I could sleep. I was thinking about going to a strange new school again, and about Papa. As for Erica, I didn't know what was keeping her awake until she asked in the darkness, "What is a quota, Lisa?"

"I think it means that only a certain number of people can get into a country at any particular time. America has a quota," I told her.

"Does Switzerland?" she asked.

"I don't know. But we can't stay here anyway."

She was silent for a time, then asked, "Have you ever seen a Nazi, Lisa?"

I sighed. "Yes."

"Are they really so terrible?"

"Yes."

Again Erica was silent, and then she sat up to look at me by the faint light that shone through the window. "Lisa," she said urgently, "I have to ask you something."

"What is it?"

"Well, I have never known anybody who was Jewish before, and it seems to me that you are—I mean," she faltered, "are all Jewish girls as good as you? And are they all so brave?"

I smiled to myself, and my heart beat faster. How strange it was that she asked me such a question, but no stranger, I realized, than my question to Mother that afternoon. I understood now why Mother had not answered. It was something I had to figure out for myself.

"Some are good and some aren't," I told Erica. I didn't say more. She would have to think it through on her own.

After a long pause Erica spoke again. "You know, Switzerland is surrounded on all sides by high mountains. The German soldiers wouldn't even try to come here. We've never been conquered. It couldn't happen."

"Of course not," I said, but to myself I thought, *Anything could happen*. Hadn't it happened in Germany?

But even at school, in the geography and history classes, the teachers spoke of Switzerland's natural barriers. When they introduced me to the class as having come from Germany, they spoke of the Nazis there, and I suppose I became somewhat of a celebrity in the little school, having escaped. At recess the other girls crowded around me, wanting to hear all about Berlin. I tried to tell them that Berlin was just a city, my home. I only wanted to remember the good things, before the Nazis. Finally the yard duty teacher came and started us all in a ball game. To me she said, "You don't have to talk about it, dear."

There was talk about Germany every night on

the radio that September. While Erica and I were doing our homework at the kitchen table, we would hear the news broadcasts in the background. Afterward Herr Werfel's face was always very grave, and he and his wife would talk together in low tones.

"It looks bad," he would say, "very bad. Hitler's going to make a grab for Czechoslovakia. The Czechs can't possibly hold out against the German army. And what next? He won't stop, that madman, until he's plunged the whole world into war."

"Maybe not," Frau Werfel replied. "Maybe other nations will help Czechoslovakia. What about England and France and even America? Don't they have treaties? Maybe, if Hitler sees they are all against him, he'll stop."

"Only force will stop him," said Herr Werfel grimly. "And that means war, world war."

I froze in my seat. America at war? How, then, could we go there? Where else in the world could we go to be safe? My imagination gave me no answers. I could only picture countries the way they looked on the large wall map at school. The black boundaries, to me, represented walls, with gates to let people in or keep them out. If there was a war, I was certain, all the gates would be closed. People did not travel freely during war. Hadn't we learned that in Germany?

All that month and into the next we waited. Even at school, where the teachers gathered in the halls to whisper together, there was a shadow over us, the same feeling we had known in Berlin. People would forget for a time and go on about their business, but then someone would ask a question or make a remark and we would remember that everyone waited, as if for a time bomb to tick to an end. And then the news changed. It was nearly winter, the news announcers said. Hitler wouldn't move in winter. He would wait at least until spring. Perhaps, they added hopefully, the big scare was over.

Mother got out of the hospital as Dr. Gross had promised and I visited her two or three times a week at the rooming house. On Sundays we were all together at the Werfels, the whole family except Papa. Annie simply went wild over the rabbits and chickens. She promptly named them all Susan.

On Sunday afternoons Frau Werfel never seemed to stop serving food, smiling and saying, "This house *should* be filled with children."

"But with such noisy children?" Mother would protest, chuckling.

"Oh, let them run and shout," Frau Werfel would say. "That's what childhood is for."

Even Ruth, who usually considered herself too grown-up for such things, romped with us in the hayloft and took leap after leap onto the stacks. She swung higher and longer than any of us on the rope swing that Herr Werfel had tied to a huge oak.

But there were other times when Ruth sat apart from us, thinking troubled thoughts, I guessed, for she wound a lock of hair around and around her finger.

"Leave Ruth alone," Mother would say, when the three of us tried to make her join in some game. "She needs some time to herself. She's growing so fast. In Berlin she would be going out with other young people, going to parties and dances."

Erica and I couldn't understand Ruth's sullen moods, or her sudden temper when we interrupted them. Once Annie, holding one of the bunnies in her arms, ran toward Ruth, who was sitting under a tree in the garden.

"Leave Ruth alone, Annie," I called teasingly. "She's in one of her 'moods' and doesn't want to be disturbed."

I knew that Ruth had heard, but she ignored me, just as she ignored Annie, who sat down beside her.

"I love it here," I heard Annie say. "Don't you love this little bunny? Don't you want to hold him?"

"No," Ruth replied shortly. "He smells."

"He smells nice," Annie insisted, burying her nose in the soft fur. "I love him. I can't take him to America, can I?"

"Of course not," Ruth retorted.

"Maybe we won't go to America," I heard Annie say. "Maybe Papa won't send for us. Maybe Papa's dead and we'll never see him again."

Suddenly Ruth's hand shot out and Annie lay screaming on the lawn. Everyone rushed over. Ruth made another grab at Annie, shaking her furiously, shouting, "She'd rather have that rabbit than ever see Papa again! She wishes Papa were dead!"

"Ruth, Ruth," Mother cried, "stop it! She's just a baby. She didn't mean that. *Leave her alone.* Just look what you've done. There, there, Annie, Ruth didn't mean it. She didn't mean it."

On Annie's cheek there was a large red mark, where Ruth's hand had struck.

"She did mean it!" Annie cried. "She hates the bunny. She hates me, too."

"No she doesn't hate anybody. She's lonesome for Papa, that's all. She's upset from waiting and wondering." I knew that Mother was speaking more to me than to Annie. "Still, it's dreadful to make such a scene," she said to Ruth, "and especially when you are a guest here. What must Frau Werfel think?"

But Frau Werfel had gone into the house and not a word was said about the episode. It was so like her to pretend that nothing at all had happened. In all the weeks I was with them, I never saw Frau Werfel lose her composure—except one terrible day in November.

PASSPORT TO FREEDOM

WE HAD JUST SAT DOWN TO BREAKFAST early that Sunday morning when the telephone rang. Frau Werfel went to answer, looking perplexed that anyone should call so early. We all knew, I think, that something dreadful had happened, even before we heard Frau Werfel's outcry and saw her face creased with sorrow and pain.

"Oh, dear God!" I heard her exclaim. "But of course you must come to us right away, my dear Frau Platt. Let us help you. My husband will leave immediately. No, no—of course it's no trouble. We'll be there in fifteen minutes, my dear."

My heart was beating frantically. I couldn't speak. I only looked at Frau Werfel, my eyes asking the question.

"A terrible thing has happened," she said weeping, "in Germany."

Inwardly I sighed with relief. At least it wasn't Papa!

Frau Werfel's voice was choked with sobs, and she would not look at any of us. "The Nazis," she began, "they have murdered . . ."

"What is it?" her husband cried. "Tell me!"

"They have murdered many—Jews—many," came the halting reply. "We must go to Frau Platt. You girls stay here," she said, throwing off her apron and wiping her face with it. "We'll be back in half an hour. Stay here," she said again, and then in silence Erica and I went into the living room to wait.

My hands were icy cold, but I didn't notice until Erica said, "Lisa, you're shivering," and she gave me Frau Werfel's knitted shawl to put around my shoulders.

As we sat there, only one vision was fastened in my mind—not of murder, for murder is something too shocking to be realized even in the imagination—but of the young Nazis in their brown shirts and black ties, stamping through the streets singing in loud, bold voices, "When the blood of Jews . . ."

Before the Werfels' car had stopped, we were outside, and in a moment I was in Mother's arms.

"Lisa!" Through all the bad times and fearful moments, I had never seen Mother look like this. "Do you know? Did Frau Werfel tell you?"

I shook my head, and beside me Frau Werfel murmured, "No. I couldn't."

"Come inside, Lisa." For several long moments Mother could not seem to begin. I only looked at her, waiting, not wanting to hear, yet needing to know.

"Lisa, there is no way I can prepare you," Mother said. "Your Uncle Arnold is dead. And Tante Helga too."

"How?" My voice sounded strange to my own ears, hollow and high.

"The Nazis."

"No." Again that toneless voice. "You must be wrong, Mother." I shook my head and covered my ears. It's a mistake, something inside me cried; it's someone else she's talking about, not my Aunt Helga, not Uncle Arnold. I love them, and they're alive, *alive*.

"It's true. Lisa, my darling come here to me, please."

But I couldn't move. Helga, my beautiful aunt who was always so gay, making jokes even on the day of parting.

"I know what you are feeling," I heard Mother's voice as from a distance, "and I cannot spare you the pain. You would know someday, you would hear of it. Look at me, Lisa! Grandmother telephoned me from Berlin. They didn't suffer, Lisa. Remember that. It was fast, and it is over for them."

Mother must have telephoned Ruth, for later she came, and we all sat together in the parlor, and through that whole long day I could not get warm, even when I stood by the fire wrapped in the knitted shawl. Late in the afternoon the sun came out, but still the room seemed gray and dim. Somewhere people were going on about their ordinary day, making plans, doing work, and taking pleasures. But for us time had stopped, and we stood still looking backward, only backward to this thing that had happened even without our knowing.

Yesterday. It was yesterday, and I was playing then, playing ball with Erica, while in Berlin the madness had already begun. Little by little, then over and over again it was told, as if by telling we could understand. It had begun with a small, angry mob, rampaging through the streets, smashing windows, smearing paint on doors and windows, hurling bricks. As night fell there were more men in the streets, some with guns, some with knives, and some with kerosene.

But there had to be a *reason*. It couldn't just have begun so suddenly, this killing of Jews.

Mother told us, and we heard it again and again on the radio all through the day. "A German official was killed in Paris. The Nazis have taken vengeance on the Jews in Germany."

Because someone in Paris had been shot, Uncle Arnold and Aunt Helga had paid with their lives. All our talk about it still left us with the same impossible question: "*Why?*"

They didn't suffer. Someone had thrown a home-made bomb into their house. An explosion ended everything. But how could we be sure? How many moments are there between life and death?

"Just believe it, Lisa," Mother said, holding me close. "It was fast and final. We will learn to live with this, somehow."

That night I went back with Mother to the rooming house, but the next day I returned to school and to the Werfels. I was glad for the routine of school, for the girls all around me at recess, and for Erica with me after school and in the evening. I did not want to be alone or idle, but at night there were always those minutes before sleep, when I had to think of it.

On one of Mother's Sunday visits to the Werfels, she brought me another letter from Rosemarie. This time the postmark was English. I tore open the letter. It was dated two weeks past, just before that terrible time in Berlin. They were safe, then! They had left in time!

I read the words hastily, then again, and wordlessly I handed the letter to Mother, looking over her shoulder to see the words once more, for Rosemarie and her sister were in England, all alone.

We have been here nearly a week, both my sister and I. Father could not bring himself to leave, with so many people needing him. My parents decided, at last, to send us to England, and we are at a kind of boarding school here. It's very crowded, but the ladies in charge are nice to us, although only one of them speaks German, and when she is not here I feel lost. So I will have to learn to speak English, just like you, Lisa, when you get to America.

"She doesn't say anything about her parents!" I cried out to Mother.

"She says that they will send for her when it's safe," Mother replied quietly.

"But what if it isn't safe? What if there *is* a war?"

"Then they will go to her in England," Mother said.

"But, Mother, it's awful for Rosemarie—she's so alone!"

"She has her sister," Mother said, "and thank God she's out of danger. Her parents did what they had to do. It isn't easy for a mother to send her child away." Her voice broke, and then she said, "We've been very lucky, Lisa. We've been able to stay together, at least in the same city."

I answered Rosemarie that night, sitting over my letter for over an hour. I told her about Erica and the farm and the school, avoiding any mention of Tante Helga or what had happened in Berlin.

Just a few days later came the message we had

been waiting for. "There's a telegram from Papa!" Mother told me joyously over the telephone. "He has sent the last form. We can buy our boat tickets!"

Mother had an appointment to see the American consul the following day, and I begged her to let me go with her. She came for me that afternoon.

"Lisa's my adventurer," she told Frau Werfel, smiling broadly. "She wants to know everything that's going on."

"I just want to see for myself," I said. "I want to be sure it's really true."

"When do you think you will leave?" Frau Werfel asked Mother.

"It could be just a couple of weeks," Mother answered. Her whole face was radiant. "My husband has sent this form—they call it number 575—to Zurich. Now all we have to do is get our passports and ship reservations."

"What a grand day for you!" Frau Werfel exclaimed. "Tonight we'll have chocolate cake to celebrate," she said to me.

In the office of the American consul we waited. I was used to waiting, and it was easy now, for I felt that here in this office we were already halfway to America.

"Margo Platt!" a clerk called out suddenly, and we jumped up. A young secretary led the way. "You have only ten minutes," she said, then opened the door to a warm, comfortable room with deep leather chairs and a highly polished desk. Behind it sat the consul, a broad-shouldered, full-faced man with crisp dark hair.

He looked up, then rose to shake Mother's hand. "Sit down, please," he said, smiling at me.

In one corner of the room stood the American flag and above it hung a picture of the president. All the while Mother and the consul were talking, I looked at that flag and the picture.

"You like that flag, don't you?" the consul said suddenly, and I blushed.

"Yes," I said softly. "And the man in the picture, the president. Do you know him? He looks so—so kind."

The man chuckled, and in place of the weariness, there was a sparkle in his eyes. "I can't say that I know him personally, but I know enough about him to tell you honestly, yes, he is kind."

"When can we go to America?" I asked, and Mother motioned to me and said, "Shh."

The man folded his hands together and faced Mother. "We have a problem," he said.

"A problem?" Mother echoed.

"Form 575," he stated. "Maybe you weren't informed, but unless we have it we can't give you a passport, Frau Platt. Now, you must write to your husband and tell him to send . . ."

"But he *has* sent it!" Mother exclaimed. "He sent me a telegram telling me that he sent the form two weeks ago, and that everything is ready now."

"My secretary has checked the files," he said, shaking his head slowly, "and we have no such form for you."

I felt that I had been running hard and couldn't

quite catch my breath. I wanted to tell him that of course Papa had sent it if he said he did! Papa would never make a mistake like that.

"All I can suggest," said the consul, "is that you have your husband send another form."

"But that might take weeks," Mother objected, "and I know he sent it. It *must* be here. We've been apart for ten months already, nearly a year, and all this time he's worked and saved and we have waited . . ."

"Please, calm yourself, Frau Platt," he said, half rising from his chair. "We are trying to do all we can. Please understand. Hundreds of people come through this office every day, hundreds of papers are sent. We don't have enough help, and everybody wants to leave immediately. I'm helpless without that form. I have to follow regulations. If it were up to me . . ."

"I'm sorry," Mother said more calmly, "but I know that somewhere in this building there is a form for us. Please, please look again."

"Very well," the man sighed. "I suppose we could check. I'll call you."

"No," Mother said, her eyes blazing with determination. "We'll wait in the other room."

"But it could take hours, or even days."

"We'll wait."

We waited. "What if they close?" I asked Mother.

"We'll wait."

I knew better than to argue when I saw the determined look in her eyes.

It was nearly five o'clock when once more the secretary called us and we were shown into the consul's office.

"You were right," he declared, beaming. "Your form was in another part of the office. What can you expect, with all this confusion? Well, now all you have to do is get some photographs of your children and yourself, and then you shall have your passports."

"Oh, good heavens, I forgot all about that," Mother groaned.

"One more day won't really matter," the consul said, smiling. "You can have it done first thing in the morning, and by noon you'll have your passports in your hands."

The next morning we were waiting outside the door when the photographer opened his shop. We waited impatiently as purposefully, slowly, he drew up the shades, turned on the lights, and unlocked the door. He was a small man, hardly taller than I, with thin stooped shoulders and a stiff mustache.

"We must have passport photographs immediately," Mother told him, when we were shown inside.

He took off his glasses and began to wipe them slowly with a tiny piece of cloth, over and over again. "No, you cannot. You cannot have them until—well, perhaps near the end of the week," he said, lingering over each word.

"Come now," Mother said pleasantly, "it must be a fairly simple process. Don't you develop the pictures right here?"

"Oh yes, that we do," the man replied. "I have all the newest equipment—yes, I have a darkroom, just newly outfitted. Would you like to see?"

Mother sighed and gave a helpless look at the ceiling.

"We must have the pictures today," she repeated. She reached inside her purse, took out a bill, and pressed it into the man's hand. "Perhaps you can make an exception and have the pictures ready today. You see, these children have not seen their father for a very long time."

"Ah, well, so," the man mused, "I suppose it could be done. I do suppose I could—try. But at least two hours. Absolutely, I cannot do it any faster."

"Fine," Mother said, smiling.

Each of us in turn sat on the high stool that stood in front of a large white screen, waiting while the photographer fussed over his lights and his camera until finally he was satisfied.

With Annie he spent so much time trying to get

her to smile, wriggling his fingers and clicking his tongue, that I blurted out, "Honestly, Annie, if you don't smile I'm going to shake you!"

Annie gave me the funniest, silliest grin I have ever seen, but the photographer thought it was perfect, and he let the lens click.

While we waited, we walked until we were shivering with cold. It had snowed in the night, not heavily, but enough to leave mounds of snow against the buildings.

"Let's make a snowman," Mother said suddenly, and I stopped to stare at her. "Right here?" I asked. "On the street?"

"Why not?" she said, laughing. "Come on. Don't be so stuffy, Lisa!"

Annie and Ruth had already begun, and although we had no mittens, we rushed to form the snow into a huge ball, patting it down, adding more, until our man was as tall as Mother.

"We need eyes," Mother directed. "Annie, find

some little pebbles. Look, we'll use this twig. It's his cigar!" She took off her brown felt hat and put it on the snowman's head and stood back, laughing.

Since we had left Germany, I had not seen Mother so gay.

People stopped to smile as they went by, and several nodded. *"Grüss Gott!"*

It ended, of course, with Ruth and Annie and I throwing snowballs at each other, and even Mother tossed a few, one landing right on my head. I laughed until my eyes were blurred. It was so funny to see Mother standing there, wearing her prim traveling suit, but her hair flying in all directions, and her hat crumpled under her arm, sending snowballs flying with perfect aim.

I wondered what the photographer must have thought of us when we returned to the shop, our clothes damp and rumpled, all of us still laughing.

Our photographs were ready. Outside, Mother opened the small envelope to see our pictures. "They do resemble us," Mother said, laughing again, "but what expressions!" Then, neatly folded among the photographs, Mother found the bill she had given the photographer to encourage him to hurry.

"How very nice of him," she exclaimed.

"Shouldn't we go back and thank him?" I suggested.

Mother paused, then shook her head. "No," she said. "I don't think he would like that. He wanted me to find the money later."

"Everybody is nice to us," Annie said, beaming.

"You be nice in the consul's office," Mother told her, "and don't chatter."

But the moment we entered the office, Annie ran around the desk, and the consul held out his arms and took her onto his lap.

"Can I go to America now?" Annie asked. "Can I see my Papa?"

"And who are you, miss?" the consul asked with mock surprise.

"Annie Platt. My Papa's waiting for me in America.

But," she added soberly, "I don't think I remember his face."

"I'm sure he remembers yours," the consul said.

He took up four slim green books and handed them to Mother. "Your passports, Frau Platt," he said, smiling. "You're on your way."

Mother held the passports tightly in her hand and looked at them for a long moment before she put them in her purse.

"Do you know," she said softly, "how it feels to have these in my hands?"

He nodded. "I know."

We had all supposed that we would leave on the very next ship, but it was already filled, and the next one too. We were to wait five more weeks, until the middle of January.

"That means you'll be here for Christmas!" Erica said happily, and for days before the holiday Frau Werfel baked and cleaned and hustled off to town, returning with gaily wrapped packages. With Herr

Werfel, Erica and I went to the edge of a pine grove to cut down the Christmas tree. On Christmas Eve, Mother and Ruth and Annie and I helped the Werfels trim the tree. It was a new experience for me, since we do not celebrate Christmas. But we all knew the Christmas carols and sang them together, watching the candles shine on the beautiful tree.

"It's good to have you with us," I heard Frau Werfel say to Mother, and Mother nodded.

"We are lucky," she said. "So many people have helped us."

There were gifts for everyone, cologne for Mother, and for me and Ruth, matching sweaters of light blue with a white snowflake design. For Annie there was a doll with real hair.

"What are you going to name her?" we all asked, laughing.

"This one," she said promptly, "will be *Erica*."

At school I had made felt bookmarks for everyone, cut into animal shapes with beads for eyes. Frau

Werfel's was in the shape of a poodle, with tufts of black wooly curls.

"I'll always treasure this, Lisa," she said softly. "Someday you'll come back to Switzerland, I hope. Maybe you'll be grown up then. What a wonderful reunion we'll have, eh? And you'll see, I'll still have your lovely gift."

The next day we went to visit Erica's aunt, and she had a present for me too, a little pocket diary bound in red leather. "This new year will be one adventure after the other for you," she said. "You'll have much to tell in your diary."

All the months away from Papa I had thought only of seeing him again, but as the day of leaving drew closer, I realized how hard it would be say good-bye once more. In America I would be truly a foreigner. How would I speak to the people there? In Switzerland we were at least familiar in language, and we were near enough to Germany to telephone.

Mother did telephone Berlin the day before we were to leave. She called from the Werfels' house, telling me in a casual tone, "I just want to talk to my mother again before we sail." From the other room I heard her speaking, and she said again and again, "Yes, truly I will send for you, Mother. Yes, of course you'll be able to leave. It won't be difficult, since I'll be in America already. Now don't you worry, Mother. I'll send for you. Good-bye, Mother. Good-bye."

For a long time afterward Mother walked by herself in the garden. I wanted to go to her, but Frau Werfel stopped me gently with a hand on my shoulder. "I think your mother would like to be alone with her thoughts for a while, Lisa."

I knew what she must be thinking. Every minute on that ocean liner would take us farther away from the danger that awaited Europe, taking us to safety, with no help to give those who stayed behind.

ARE YOU
MY PAPA?

DURING THE LAST WEEK BEFORE WE LEFT,
Frau Werfel sat for hours at her sewing machine,
and when it was time to pack, my suitcase was filled
with new clothes. Everything I had brought from
Germany was threadbare, except for my coat. On the
last day Herr Werfel took me to Zurich to buy new
shoes, sturdy brown oxfords and also a pair of white
party slippers.

"But do you think I'll need party shoes?" I asked
hesitantly.

"A young lady like you?" he said. "Of course!"

Annie, too, was newly outfitted, and when we all

met at the station, I saw to my surprise that Ruth was wearing silk stockings and shoes with a slight heel. She wore a new traveling suit, and her hair had been cut and curled. My sister, incredibly, my sister had grown up, and I hadn't even noticed! It seemed so strange to see her like this, more absorbed than ever with her own thoughts; and when she said good-bye to the Kunst family, I saw the boy lean toward her briefly for a kiss.

The railroad station was filled with the commotion of arrivals and partings. Great engines steamed, and their shrill whistles pierced the air, while the loudspeaker rumbled continually, "Last call . . . train for Paris leaving on track 17 . . . all aboard, please. All aboard."

"Grüss Gott! Grüss Gott!" Our Swiss friends kissed us good-bye, and just before I mounted the high iron steps of the train, Frau Werfel pressed a large box of chocolates into my hands.

I saw Erica waving as the train moved down the

track, and I waved back until she was out of sight. Annie chattered to herself as she looked through her new picture book, but for Mother and Ruth and me there was nothing we could say. I took out my little diary and wrote, "At last we are on our way to America." I looked at the words, repeated them to myself, but I felt no excitement and no joy—only a great lump in my throat.

I slept and awakened to the confusion of another arrival.

"We're in Paris!" Ruth cried, shaking me. "Oh, I can't wait to see it. Will we see the Eiffel Tower?" she asked Mother. "Oh, I want to see everything. I've heard it's so beautiful."

To me it was just the same as any railroad station—dirty and old and busy, and the many porters sped right past us, although Mother signaled and tried to speak in her halting French. At last Mother caught the arm of one of the porters and showed him an address that someone from the ticket office had scribbled on a piece of paper.

The man glanced at the note, nodded briskly, and scooped up our bags. We ran behind him and soon found ourselves in a bus filled with travelers.

The sun was just setting, and Ruth and I strained to see the sights, crowding together at the window. "Can't we get off, Mother?" she begged. "Can't we *see* Paris? What good is it looking from a window?"

"We're not in Paris for sightseeing, Ruth," Mother said. "We're to go to a special place overnight, and tomorrow morning we'll take the train to Le Havre. Oh, Ruth, don't be disappointed. Just think, we're sailing tomorrow!"

But Ruth was scowling, and suddenly she gave me a sharp pinch and grumbled, "Quit pushing, Lisa. Honestly, you're a pest."

Mother gave me a warning look. *Don't fight,* it said, *not now.* I moved away from the window.

The bus stopped beside a row of flat wooden buildings, like army barracks, set in a grim, dusty enclosure of wire fencing.

"It looks like a prison!" Ruth gasped as we followed the others through the narrow corridors of the building.

"This room." Someone pointed, and we went in.

Inside there were three iron beds, each covered with a single army blanket. There was nothing else in the room, no chair, no shelf, only a bulb hanging down from a long black wire to show the raw timbers of the walls.

"I'm freezing," Ruth muttered.

"Can't you stand it for one night?" Mother demanded.

We lined up to receive our supper: a stew of potatoes and green beans with slivers of meat. After that we lined up again for the washroom. People did not speak to each other or introduce themselves. By tomorrow they would be strangers again, sailing on different ships to different places.

Annie slept with me, and we kept each other warm by huddling close together. We were awakened by a sharp blast, like a factory whistle, and I jumped out into the cold.

Mother was already dressed, and she hastily packed our pajamas. "Hurry!" she told us repeatedly. "Ruth, hurry up. Stop combing your hair, for goodness' sake. Lisa, help Annie get dressed."

Annie was still half asleep, and I had to push and pull to get her clothes on, for she kept popping her thumb back into her mouth. As soon as we were on the bus, Annie began to wail. "I have to go to the bathroom!"

"You can't. You'll have to wait," I told her, "until we're on the train."

It was still pitch-black outside, and it felt as if we were driving through a tunnel all the way to the station. In the train there were dim night-lights.

It was a short ride to Le Havre, where the ship waited. Again we were in a huge station room, and again our luggage and papers had to be inspected.

"I'll never travel again," Ruth mumbled, "never. I've

had enough. It's nothing but waiting and getting up at the crack of dawn to go to another waiting room."

I had never seen so many people rushing and shouting, all carrying bundles. Even the little children were laden with bags and boxes—Annie, too, with her dolls and things.

"I want to go see the ship," Annie said, hopping up and down impatiently.

"We have to wait here for Mother," I told her. "Just sit down."

Through the windows I could see the huge ship bobbing up and down like a giant cork in the gray water. I could see barrels and boxes being brought up the ramp, and others being hoisted aboard with a huge crane. "Just look at it," I said. "Look, Annie."

Annie! She had been there, right beside me! "Ruth, where's Annie?" I shouted above the noise.

Ruth stared at me. "*Where? You* were watching her. I don't know where she went. Why didn't you watch her? Why didn't you hold on to her?" Her voice rose sharply, and I strained to see through the crowds, my panic mounting. How, among all those people, could we find her? And Mother—what would I say to Mother?

"Find her! Find her!" Ruth shouted at me.

"Maybe she's at the candy stand," I said, steadying my voice. "I'll go and look."

"No! Mother told us to . . ."

"You stay here and tell her . . . tell her."

I broke away and rushed over to the candy stand, but no Annie. I called, but my voice was lost in the sounds of other voices, and when I came back to Ruth, Mother was standing beside her, her face white and hard.

"*You two sit here*," she said, "and this time obey me!"

I wanted to explain. She had been there and then she was gone. I wanted to tell Mother I was sorry, for all the good that would do!

"Just stay here. I'll find her," Mother said.

"They'll sail without us," Ruth said over and over

again while we waited. "They won't wait. I knew something like this would happen."

I tried to concentrate on looking for Annie, and on
ignoring Ruth's accusing moans. "They'll sail without
us. It's all your fault."

At last I couldn't bear it and I wanted to shake Ruth
with all my might. "Stop it!" It was not a shout, although
inside I felt that I was bursting. "You are the oldest. Just
stop that awful moaning and behave yourself!"

She only gasped, and in that instant Mother was
beside us, grasping Annie tightly by the arm. Annie
was silent, red-eyed, sniffling only a little, and rub-
bing the place where she had been spanked.

"Now," Mother said, drawing a deep breath, "we
will go to the ship."

Our ship was a large French ocean liner, as large as
several city blocks, and in every way like a whole town
afloat. Whatever we wanted, there it was: games on
the deck, meals we had once dreamed about, music in
the lounge at night, and dancing. There were movies,

and we all went to see them at night, even Annie. They were the first films I had seen in nearly a year, wonderful, funny films and stories that I loved.

It was like one long vacation from day to day, until on the fifth day the air grew cold, the wind began to blow, whistling along the deck, and the ship tipped and swayed from side to side.

Annie thought it was a joke to try to walk on the rolling, pitching deck, until at lunch she became very pale and whispered, "I think I'm going to be sick."

"Nonsense," Mother said quickly, giving her a piece of bread to eat. "You're just hungry. Only babies get seasick."

I didn't say anything, but it was clear by the empty places in the dining room that nearly half the passengers couldn't face the thought of a meal, and even as we ate our lunch others left hastily, their hands over their mouths.

At the evening meal only a handful of people appeared. Glasses slid clear across the table. We clutched at the handrails as we walked, sometimes being tilted from one side of the passageway to the other.

Everywhere there was talk of the storm, and passengers crowded around the purser's desk, anxiously wanting to know when it would end, when we would arrive in America. A sign was posted announcing a delay in our arrival. We would be a whole day late, due to the storm, and maybe two.

All the next day the wind blew in fierce gusts, and by noon Ruth lay in her bunk, unable to rise. "Go away," she moaned. "I can't eat. Go away. I'm dying."

"Seasick," Mother said lightly; and Annie sang out, "Only babies get seasick, Ruth," whereupon Ruth threw down a slipper, which Annie dodged.

Again we stood at the purser's desk, and this time the people were all talking at once, frantic about the delay. Two elderly women were in a state of near hysteria. "We'll sink, I know it," one cried out.

And the other wept, "How can fate be so cruel? We'll never see America. Never."

"I'd like to send a message," Mother told the purser when our turn had come. "My husband will be planning to meet the ship, and I want to tell him about the delay."

"I'm sorry," said the purser. "We cannot send any private messages. Your husband will probably be in touch with the steamship company, or he will find out through the newspapers."

"He'll check with the company," I told Mother. "Papa always checks things like that. Don't worry."

"I hope so," Mother said, frowning. Then she smiled at me. "You're right, dear. It's silly to fret about it."

By morning the winds had settled, the sea was calm. People began to sit on the deck again. The next day, it was said, the next day we would see land.

Night brought a change in mood, a great excitement, an air of celebration. People danced in the dining room and the ship's orchestra played gay tunes, while newly found friends exchanged addresses.

The next morning everyone was up early, crowding

at the rails, straining to see the first glimpse of land. We stood close together, the four of us, and several times there was a false cry—land!—then disappointment and Annie's questions: "When? When?"

For nearly two hours we stood. Then, suddenly there began a murmur, rising to a shout, until it spread the length and breadth of the ship. "America! America! I see it! Look!"

People shouted wildly as they pressed closer and closer to the rail to see the dim, distant outline of the Statue of Liberty. Parents held their little children high on their shoulders that they might see, and I strained on tiptoe, shouting at the top of my lungs while I stared at the statue and the buildings in the distance, thinking it might be a dream, but the throbbing inside me was real, very real.

"I'll never forget this sight," Mother whispered.

Beside us an old woman wept, her head pressed against her husband's shoulder. "America! God be praised!"

On and on, the shouting, the waving, the tears. The ship seemed to rock and sway with it, and then I heard the first strains of music from the ship's orchestra. If people didn't know the words, they sang the tune, "America! America! God shed His grace on thee."

Amid the streaming crowd we made our way down the gangplank, and when we stood on firm ground, my legs still swayed from the motion of the sea. I saw a bearded young man beside me stoop down and gather up a handful of soil, and everything he felt showed in his eyes.

For a few moments we stood lost in the tangle of people, all waiting for someone, all wondering where to go. We began to walk, following painted arrows. We passed through many rooms and saw many people who looked at our papers, and then, suddenly, Mother stopped short.

I can't remember what I said or did, but I heard the shriek from Ruth, and I suppose my own voice mingled with hers, "Papa! Papa!" It was as if I had been hurled through space and dropped here, straight into Papa's arms.

With all the crowd milling past, Mother and Papa drew close in a long embrace. At last Papa exclaimed, "Annie, darling, don't you know me?" For Annie hung back, clutching Mother's hand.

Now Annie came forward and said with a strange, shy look, "Are you my Papa? Are you really?"

"Oh yes, my little Annie! I am, and I love you." Papa scooped her up into his arms, and Annie buried her face in his neck. "Yes," she sighed. "Oh, Papa!"

"Come now," Papa said, with his arm around me. "There's time for talk later. I want to hear everything. But now," he said, his voice husky, "let's go home. It's just a little apartment, and I don't have much furniture yet."

"It will be beautiful," Mother whispered.

Home, I thought, *home was a feeling more than a place.* I gave Papa's hand a squeeze and he smiled down at me. Yes, we were home.

AFTERWORD

JOURNEY TO AMERICA IS MY TRUE STORY, begun many years ago. But the memory has never left me.

As the years went by I came to understand my mother's courage and sacrifice, and I was amazed. Mother made the plan for our escape, sending Father out first, because the Nazis were taking Jewish men from their homes at night. She remained in Germany with me and my two older sisters until Father could send for us. It took a year for us to be reunited. My mother's decision to leave was what saved us. She saw the signs of disaster very clearly. She had "street smarts," knowing what was important, when to take risks. And it was risky and lonely to go to a strange place without money or family or friends, unable to speak the language. This is what immigrants have always done, and many are still doing it today as they flee from persecution and war.

Mother always said, "Only in America!" when it came to freedom and opportunities. She took it as her duty to work at the local election board. In later years she often went to the senior citizens center for lunch. Sometimes an entertainer came to lead a sing-along. Mother would stand up as tall as her five feet allowed, calling out, "We should sing 'God Bless America.'" They did. Sometimes I see films of little children fleeing from guns and tanks and soldiers. And I think, that might have been me if my mother hadn't made the choices she made. For me, it has been a very good life in America.

Mother commiserated with the poor, even when we were poor ourselves. She sent packages back to friends in war-torn Germany, filled with cocoa, coffee, hard candies, sardines, tins of biscuits. Mother included woolen scarves and socks she had knitted. The letters of thanks came weeks later, filled with joy.

Mother never passed a beggar on the street without giving a coin or a dollar. When I was little, she would hand me the money and direct me to put it into the beggar's cup. She gathered up clothes and shoes and took them to the needy. If she heard a nasty remark about someone's religion or race, she spoke up. Once, standing in line for a movie, she heard someone make a racist slur. "You are a Nazi!" she screamed into the woman's face. She was not timid when it came to fighting prejudice.

Today, we know that the world is still struggling with prejudice and poverty and war. Everyone cannot be a superhero, nor can any one person change the world. But small acts of kindness, taken together, can do great things.

Now fifty years have passed since *Journey to America*

was first published. It has become part of my life's journey, allowing me to travel and meet many people, to speak to groups of children and adults. The meaning of my life has been to teach, both in the classroom and through my books. I want to be a bridge between people, from past to present, and to shine a light on different countries and cultures. This, I believe, is the road to peace.

My mother lived to be ninety-six years old. Toward the end her memory failed. But she always remembered one thing very clearly. "I came to America with three children and ten dollars."

And she gave away copies of *Journey to America* to everyone she met.

An unforgettable, inspiring story of hope and innocence and one family's miraculous survival

Looking for another great book?
Find it
IN THE MIDDLE.

Fun, fantastic books for kids
in the in-be**TWEEN** age.

IntheMiddleBooks.com

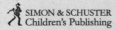